MOUNT ZION PLAYS

DARKEST NIGHT

(A Night of Final Decision)

And its Poetic Embrace by
Olumide Oki

MIKE BAMILOYE

Darkness Night 2
Copyright © 2024 by Mike Bamiloye. All rights reserved.

No part of this publication may be reproduced, stored in a retrieval system, or transmitted in any way by any means, electronic, mechanical, photocopy, recording, or otherwise without the prior permission of the author except as provided by USA copyright law.

The opinions expressed by the author are not necessarily those of Veritas Ink and Press

Veritas Ink and Press is committed to excellence in the publishing Industry.

Book Design copyright 2024 by Mike Bamiloye. All Rights Reserved.

Published in the United States of America

ISBN : 979-8-8692-4785-8
eISBN : 979-8-8692-4786-5

Dedication

"All over the World are Children if the Kingdom passing through different persecutions and tribulations….This message here is dedicated to all the Standing Ones.

All over the World are Believers facing difficult times for their Faith in the Christ that died for them…To them all, this dramatic piece is humbly dedicated.

May the Lord empower them all. May the Lord strengthen them all. May they all stand for HIM till the end to take their Crowns of Overcomers.

May we all Stand for Him who died for us."

Section One

THE DRAMA

Mike Bamiloye

Introduction

"If you come face to face with these situations, what would you do?"

This solemn question is what the author has brought before the readers of this heart-searching play. Would you turn your back in the Darkest Night or would you take your stand for your faith?

This play is neither a recount of past or current events, but a mirror of possible occurrence at any time and any place.

We hear of many incidences of persecution and tribulation occurring in many parts of the world. We heard of a great number of believers being carted away in trucks to be slaughtered for their faith.

We read of occurrences of violent persecutions of the Christians in many parts of the world, while in other sections of the world, life is going normally in a multi-religious society. Could it be that the Christians living in persecuted environments are stronger in faith than the Christians in secular-religious tolerant nations?

Can many Churches and Believers in many free nations enjoying the freedom of their faith presently stand in the face of violent persecutions?
Would many still stand in the face of death? Won't many deny their faith when faced with agony and death for their faith?

This play is a mirror of probability. What if? Would you still stand? Can you die for what you believe?

May this reasoning arouse in you an urgency for a rededication of life.

Mike Bamiloye
March 2022

Scene One

There is chaos and pandemonium everywhere. Sporadic gunshots and screams pervade the air. Stampedes and wailings. It is night of sorrow and tears.

A band of religious extremists had invaded a small community of Agbamu, a small town near the Federal Capital Territory of the nation. Men, women, children, and elderly are seen running in different directions panicky. The gunshots continue tearing the dead night amid the noisy screaming and the groaning of the dying and the wounded.

A man, Kenny, leads his wife, Tobi and three children into an uncompleted building in fear and tears. Tobi trying to cover the mouth of the panicking youngest, and Kenny holding the two other children to his bosom, panting heavily in sweat and tears.

KENNY: (*to his wife*) Sweet-Heart, the Lord shall deliver us... the Lord shall deliver us! The Lord God Almighty shall deliver us...! No evil shall befall us!

TOBI: (*frightened, talking breathlessly in fear*) Honey... Ah! They killed Bro. Joel! They killed Bro. Joel! I saw him fell...! Bullets hit him...! Bullet hit him...! (*crying*) Ah! Bro Joel... Ah...!

KENNY: (*speaking in lower tone*) Sh-h-h-h-h! Calm down...! Kenny,

Calm...down! Sh-h-h-h! Quiet...! Footsteps approaching! (*whispers*) Coming towards here...

CHILD I: (*shaking in the embrace of his father. Whispering*) Ah! They've found us...! They are coming for us. ....!

KENNY: (*hush tones*) No! Just be quiet!

(*They all crawl to the dark side of the room and remain quiet. Shortly, a man is pushed into the adjacent room, where the family can have a clearer focus of him from inside their dark hiding place. And they can clearly hear all conversations between them. They withdraw further, shaking and sticking to the wall as they hear all their conversation. Two men follow the man into the place with their guns held dangerously at the man whose mouth and nose are dripping blood. One of the gunmen pushes him to the wall*)

GUNMAN I: (*to the man*) So, where are you running to?

GUNMAN II: (*pointing the gun at him, now, at closer range*) Enough of all jokes, we have no patience with a man who drags matter unnecessarily long. Say your last prayers or accept to denounce your faith and religion! (*They cock the gun*)

THE MAN: (*talks in fear*) Eh-eh! No! No! Please. Don't shoot! Don't shoot! Wait! Wait

GUNMAN I: We have no pleasure in patience! Talk quick!

THE MAN: (*weeping and stammering*) Ah... What should I say, sir?

GUNMAN II: Who is Jesus to you?

THE MAN: He is.. .He is...the Son...the Son...

GUNMAN I: (*shouts at him*) Don't...Don't..! Don't you dare say that! That is what we don't want to hear! Just say Jesus is the Son of God and you are dead! And just say: Jesus is not the Son of God, and you would not follow him again...

THE MAN: (*shivering in fear and tears*) Ah! Ah! Jesus..Eh! (*They cock the gun, ready to shoot*)

GUNMAN II: What a nonsense! Your time is up, Mr. Man. What is your name?

THE MAN: Joel, Sir. I am Joel...Ah! Please! Don't kill me!

GUNMAN II: I will give you to the count of five to make up your mind or say goodbye to the world: One.... Two...

THE MAN: (*shivering and breathing heavily*) Ah! Jesus Christ...! Show up yourself now...! Save me now!

GUNMAN II: ....Three...!

THE MAN: You said you would deliver us from all evil... you said...

GUNMAN II: ... Four...!

THE MAN: You said, call upon me and I will answer you. .... I am
calling...now... Please, answer me now...

GUNMAN II: Time up now, man. ....(*Steadies his gun and raises it at
him*)

THE MAN: (*shouts aloud*) Oh! No! Wait! Wait!

GUNMAN I: (*impatiently*) Wha-a-at! You are wasting our time!

THE MAN: What should I say? Tell me what to say. (*Gunman II brings out a piece of paper from his back pocket, unfolds it and begins to read it*)

GUNMAN II: Now kneel and say this Prayer of Confession after me. Quick! (*The Man goes on his knees slowly*) And say after me: Jesus Christ

THE MAN: Jesus Christ.................!

GUNMAN II: I renounce you today as my Lord and Saviour!

THE MAN: What?

GUNMAN II: You heard me, or should I repeat myself?

THE MAN: Yes, sir!

GUNMAN II: Jesus Christ...!

THE MAN: Jesus Christ...!

GUNMAN II: I renounce you today as my Lord and Saviour!

THE MAN: (*Quietly sobbing. Then, he looks up and wipes his eyes.*) I. I accept you today as my Lord and Saviour!

GUNMAN I: (*shouts madly*) Are you deaf? You are deaf? "Renounce!" not "Accept"

GUNMAN II: (*re-cocks his gun and points it at his head now?*) I renounce you today as my Lord and Saviour! Say it!

THE MAN: (*closes his tearful eyes and breathes heavily*) I accept You today as my Lord and Saviour!

GUNMAN II: So be it then. Go and meet your Jesus in Hell.

THE MAN: Jesus is not in Hell, sir, He is in Heaven. He is waiting for me in Paradise; He is waiting for my arrival. Jesus! Jesus! I have not denied you ooo. I didn't t say what they said I should say ooo! I didn't renounce You... I said I accept You... Please, forgive all my sins ooo. You are my saviour ooo!

(*Gunman I shoot point blank, his blood splattered on the wall as he crumbles on the ground, dead. Kenny and his family shiver as they watch this incidence from the dark corner of the place. They shake in fear and apprehension. The children are crying frightfully in silence. The Gunmen go out of the building into the open space where some people are being shot and some are knelling renouncing their faith*).

TOBI: (**panicking nervously, tears**) Sweet-Heart, what shall we do?
What's going to happen to us?

KENNY: (*to the children*) Now, listen, Children! Be calm. The Lord is with us! Esther.

ESTHER: (*crying*) Yes, Dad...I am scared. They are going to kill us.

KENNY: No, they would not kill us...! Don't say things like that. You must be bold for your siblings.

TOBI: (*tearfully*) Ah...! Jesus! (*She moves to peep through a small opening on the wall and pulls back with fright and shock*) Ah! Kenny! Kenny...! Jeesus!

KENNY: What....?

TOBI: (*breathlessly in whisper*) Someone is coming... Someone is... Jesus! (*They all shrink back into the dark, trembling.*)

KENNY: (*with shaking whispering voice*) Now listen, every one of you...No fear. No panic. Esther, Kola, Lanre, calm down and listen.... Don't ever deny Jesus Christ...He will not allow us to die...He will Protect us. But...if anything happens, don't ever deny Christ.

TOBI: (*grabs her husband's arm, trembling*) Stop talking, he is getting closer here... Sh-sh-sh... Kenny stop!

KENNY: (*continues to whisper*) We shall live and not die. But in case I got to Heaven before you all... If any of you deny Jesus Christ, you will never see me again. Ever!

TOBI: Kenny, stop!

(A man in military camouflage storms inside the room *with a gun*

*in his hand. He holds a touch-light with the other hand, pointing the
light around the place).*

Scene Two

(Somewhere in the small town. Another family are hiding in fear inside their house. The small family of Anderson comprise of four: the couple with their two grown up boy and young lady. The mother and the two children are standing by the dinning side of the living room, quivering and highly terrified. The sounds of noises, screaming and shouting are mingled with the sporadic gunshots that rent the dark night outside. Mr. Anderson rushes down the stairs into the living room.)

ANDERSON: *(with trembling voice)* Honey...we have a company. Someone has entered the compound.

MARTHA: *(nervously in low voice)* Who? Ah!

ANDERSON: I saw Simon, the Choir Leader coming towards here and... two other persons I can't recognize. Now, all of you go into the room there, and hide. I will wait for them. And don't come outside here.

MARTHA: No, I will stay. No running away anywhere...! Temmy and you Laolu, go into the room, quick...Quick, go!

(The two children rush into the room and shut the door as there is a bang on the door immediately. The bangs come repeatedly.

Anderson walks to the door cautiously and unlocks the door and opens it quietly. A young man enters, looking worried and nervous.)

SIMON: Good evening, Pastor. I am very sorry..
ANDERSON: Simon, what happened? Sorry for what?

MARTHA: Bro. Simon, where are the people that were coming with you?

SIMON: (*stammers*) That was what I was trying to say, Mummy. (*He walks back to the door and opens the door for two men who carry guns.*)

MAN I: You are Pastor Anderson, I suppose?
ANDERSON: Yes, Sir. That is correct, sir.

MAN I: We are in search of all men of God in town. We are searching for Pastors, Reverends and church leaders and their families. So, with his help, we were able to get to your house.

MARTHA: (*shocked*) What! Bro. Simon, so when you called us on phone few minutes ago, and said you wanted to check on our welfare if we are OK, and we told you we were in the house hiding, this was it right?

SIMON: I am sorry, Ma. They were with me, and they asked me to find out if you were at home and to bring them to your place. I couldn't do otherwise. Sir and Ma.

MARTHA: you couldn't do otherwise, So you betrayed us!

SIMON: (*harshly*) What could I have done, Ma? I was asked to do this at the point of gun and with a promise that I would not be killed if I obey them and bring them to you. Do you expect me to tell lies that I don't know your place? Did you teach us to tell lies? I did what I needed to do, and I am sorry, if I am wrong.

MAN II: Other Christians and especially Pastors and church leaders like you in town are being hunted down to reaffirm their religious positions and confession. If they do the right thing, they will live and if not, they would be wasted. We are presently getting rid of non-compliant and uncooperative entities, to make our world a better place to live.

MAN I: Your man here has already made a good decision to live, that is why he is living and helping us in our search of other fanatics who would be given the choices to live or be wasted.

ANDERSON: Simon, what decision have you made to live?

SIMON: Well, Sir...they simply asked from me a simple question and I gave to them correct answer.

ANDERSON: Which was...?

MAN I: Leave the question to us, Pastor Anderson. We are to ask, and you are to answer correctly if you desire to live.

ANDERSON: What question is it, sir?
MAN II: Who is Jesus Christ to you?
ANDERSON: (*dazed, he turns to Simon*) Was that the question?
MAN II: (*barks at him*) Answer the question!
ANDERSON: Ah. Well, Sir. Jesus Christ is the...Son of...!
SIMON: No-o, Pastor. Don't say it...!

ANDERSON: What, don't say what?

MAN I: (*shouts at him*) Don't you dare say that! That is what we don't want to hear. Anyone who Confesses that Jesus is the Son of God shall be killed with immediate effect and anyone who chooses to live will have to say otherwise.

ANDERSON: (*shocked*) Ahl Ahl Jesus... (*they cock the gun, ready to shoot*)

MARTHA: (*with surprise*) Bro. Simon, did you answer otherwise?
SIMON: Mummy, I had no choice, Ma.

MARTHA: You had a choice, Bro Simon!

MAN II: We should start from you, woman. Who is Jesus Christ to you?

MARTHA: (*pauses briefly in tears, then speaks*) I have gone too far....
than to now deny Him who died for me on the Cross. How can I deny the One who paid for my sins and prepare a mansion for me in Heaven?

ANDERSON: (*scared*) No, Honey, hold on.... Wait..
MARTHA: (*hotly*) Sweet-Heart, what?

MAN I: (*pointing the gun at her head*) Tango, this is time wasting! Let's be quick here and go to other places. Answer the question quick!

MAN II: (*shouts at her*) Who is Jesus to you, Woman?
MARTHA: (*shouts back at him*) I have given my answer, Gunman!

MAN II: (*shouts angrily, cocking his gun to shoot*) Who is Jesus to you?

ANDERSON: (*loudly*) No! Don't shoot! Don't shoot! Ple-asel Give us time to think about it

MARTHA: (*to her husband aloud*) Time to think about what, Honey?
What is that to think about?

ANDERSON: Honey, be patient! Use your brain! Let's be wise!

MARTHA: (*shocked*) Really? The wisest thing to do now is to stand on the side of the Lord who paid the price for your sins.

MAN II: (*angrily*) We are giving both of you up to the Count of five to give us an answer now or we take a decision for you.

(*There is a struggling sound outside the entrance door. As they turn in the direction, a young man staggers inside, covered with blood on his face and chest. He staggers forward and falls at the Pastor's feet.*)

ANDERSON: Segun! What happened?

SEGUN: (*fainting*) They stormed into our midst in the church vestry where we were hiding. They have killed Anthony and Kemi...!

MARTHA: Ye-eh! Ah!

SEGUN: They refused to renounce...they shot them... they tortured me to renounce... but I did not renounce. I stood my feet...and I escaped to come and inform you...!

ANDERSON: Ah! Jesus!

MAN II: Do you see how long you have wasted our time?

(Shortly, a security officer in uniform bursts inside. He goes to him and pulls him up away from the Andersons.)

OFFICER: *(hotly in anger)* Go on your knees! *(The man falls on his knees, in tears and exhaustion)* You have wasted my time and making me to pursue you unnecessarily. Were you running here with the hope of being saved by this man? Do you now see that our men are here already? Now the confession and renunciation! Quick! I hate wasters of precious time!

SEGUN: What should I say?

OFFICER: *(bringing out a piece of paper from his breast pocket. He unfolds it and reads)* Say after me: Jesus Christ...!

SEGUN: Jesus Christ...!
OFFICER: "I renounce you today as my Lord and Saviour...!" Say it!

SEGUN: *(looks up to the officer in his bloody face)* Look here, Officer, it is too late for that: "I have been crucified with Christ; it is no longer I who live, but Christ lives in me; and the life which I now live in the flesh I live by faith in the Son of God, who loved me and gave Himself for me." Galatians 2:20

OFFICER: *(irritated)* So, you are prepared to die?

SEGUN: (*smiles broadly with his blood-drooping mouth*) "If then you were raised with Christ, seek those things which are above, where Christ is, sitting at the right hand of God. Set your mind on things above, not on things on the earth. Colossians 3:1-2

OFFICER: So, you would rather die than renoune your faith?

SEGUN: (*shakes his heads resolutely*) Yes, sir. For have died, and my life is hidden with Christ in God. Colossians 3:3

OFFICER: If you have died, why are you still alive?
SEGUN: (*begins to sing*)
It is no longer I that liveth, but Christ that liveth in me, it is no Longer I that liveth, but Christ that liveth in me, In me, In me,

Jesus is alive in me,
It is no longer I that liveth, but Christ that liveth in me...

OFFICER: If it is no longer, you that lives, then, why wasting my time all this while.

SEGUN: (*looking up with a smile*) I see...Angels... everywhere, waiting to escort the Saints home.

OFFICER: Beautiful hallucinations! Then go and meet the angels! You fool!
(*He raises up his gun and shoots. Segun falls backward. The gunshot gives a reverberating echo enveloping the whole house. The Andersons tremble with shock. Inside the room where the Anderson children are hiding. Both are crying and nervously scared. The boy cringes fearfully at the sound of the gunshot.*)

LAOLU: (*shivering in tears*) Ah..! Temmy, they've killed Daddy and Mummy...! they shot my parents...Ah! Ah...!

TEMMY: (*shaking as she talks in low voice*) Ah! Quiet...! No..! Jesus... ! No...! It was one gunshot...! It could be Mum...or Dad...! Jesus!
(*In the living room: The motionless body of Segun lies on the floor in a pool of blood. Pastor Anderson and his wife are still on their knees before the Officer and the two Gunmen sobbing at the sight of the cruel murder they just witnessed.*)

OFFICER: (*to the kneeling couples*) We do not have time to waste, we have an order to move to another part of the town where some Christians are hiding. Have you taken their confessions?

MAN II: We are about to.
(*The Officer brings out the piece of paper from his breast pocket again, and unfold it*)

OFFICER: Very well then, can you say this after me?

MARTHA: (*defiantly*) There is nothing to say after you, Sir. As for me and my house, we shall serve the Lord!

ANDERSON: (*loudly*) Come-on, Honey, will you keep quiet and be reasonable for once!...

MARTHA: Wha-at Sweet-Heart...! What happened? Are you telling me to keep quiet? You are refraining me from standing for what we believe in and what we have preached for years?

ANDERSON: No, Martha, let's be wise here...!

MARTHA: I choose to be foolish here...when it concerns confession of my faith in the Lord Jesus Christ. Whaa-aat! Sweet-Heart, I can't believe you are saying this!

ANDERSON: (*tries to speak to her in low voice*) Can we choose to run now, in order to fight another day?

MARTHA: Why should I choose to run away from the battle on this great day the Angels of Heaven are watching the game? Segun just won his game! He fought to the very end! He is just our church worker! We taught him to stand on the day of battle. We taught him to defend his faith! We taught him to stand for Jesus Christ and never to look back! Why should we who taught him to fight the fight of faith turn back on the day of Battle?

OFFICER: (*shouts aloud*) By Order of Protocol, we are to make you recite the Confession Creed for you to decide either to live or die. Therefore, can you say this after me?

MARTHA: (*strongly*) Say it and I would say what I need to say!
OFFICER: Jesus Christ...!

MARTHA: Jesus Christ...!

OFFICER: I renounce You today as my Lord and Saviour...!

MARTHA: (*affirmatively*) I Accept You today as my Lord and Saviour...!

OFFICER: You need to say it correctly, or I would take it that you choose to die for what you believe.

MARTHA: (*boldly as tears stream down his face*) Today, Death is seen as my friend...A close friend standing between me and my glorious Eternity.

OFFICER: So, be it then, you choose to die today, right?

(Inside the room where Temmy and Laolu are hiding, they are hearing the words of their mother, as they listen with fear and tears)

TEMMY: *(speaking quietly)* That's Mum talking...

LAOLU: *(nervously)* Mum is arguing with them... Mum is not calming down with them...they would be irritated... they may get angry...

TEMMY: Listern...Listen...Laolu, listen to what Mum is saying.... they want Mum to deny Jesus, Daddy once told us. during one of the Power Nights in the church. that night there was a mighty move of God when we had a visiting minister from Kenya...

LAOLU: The man said, the Lord sent him to go all over telling God's Children, never to deny faith when persecution and tribulation arise.

TEMMY: And we shall not deny Jesus...! We shall not deny Jesus...! *(The Officer put his gun at Martha's head.)*

OFFICER: I give you to the count of three to change your mind and recite the Creed. One...!

ANDERSON: *(pleading in low voice)* Honey, please...Don't do this...!

MARTHA: (*to Anderson with a faint smile in tears*) I thought I would see you at the other side..I thought both of us would enter the Pearly Gate hand in hand...and fall into the embrace of the Master who appointed us into His vineyard...

OFFICER: Two...!

ANDERSON: (*holds her hand*) Martha...!

MARTHA: I will wait for you at the other side...if you come over there. There is nothing else here worth dying for. (*She raises up her voice aloud*)

MARTHA: To whom, it may concern! Deny not the faith and we shall meet at the other side!

(*Inside the hidden room, Temmy and Laolu are standing behind the door listening to the conversation nervously*)

TEMMY: Can you hear that Mum is talking to us...!

(*Then there is a very loud gunshot and the loud shout of Anderson follow*)

ANDERSON: Oh! No! Martha! Oh! God! Martha!

LAOLU: (*cries a bit loud*) Ah! They've killed Mummy! They've killed Mum!

(*In the living room, Martha's body lies on the floor in blood. Anderson crumbles on the floor crying.*)

OFFICER: (*looks in the direction of the room*) I heard a sound from that room. Are there other people with you in the house?

ANDERSON: (*sobbing*) No-o! No! My wife and I are the only one in the house.

OFFICER: Your wife is gone, now it's your turn to....

(*Temmy and Laolu run out of the room shouting panicky*)

TEMMY: Noo! Don't kill our dad, Ple-ase!

ANDERSON: (*tearfully*) Oh-No-o-o! Children, what have you done!
We told you to hide! What have you done?

LAOLU: We heard him saying it's your turn to die! And we don't want them to kill you.

ANDERSON: Nooo! He was saying it is my turn to make the Statement!

OFFICER: Whao! So, you have been hiding in that room. Anyone else in there?

TEMMY: Oh..! Mummy! (*She rushes to the lifeless body of her Mum in the pool of blood, crying*)

OFFICER: (*to one of the Gunmen*) You go and check through the rooms if anyone else is hiding there.

MAN I: Yes, Sir. (*He goes briskly, to check the rooms*)

OFFICER: (*to Anderson*) Now that your wife has chosen her path of dishonour, Now, it is your turn. Make it snappy to save us from unnecessary stress. Now say this after me, please. "Jesus Christ..."

ANDERSON: (*sobs*) Jesus Christ...!

OFFICER: Today, I renounce You as my Lord and Saviour....

ANDERSON: Today, I....

TEMMY: (*springs to her feet in anger*) No-o-o! Daddy! You can't do that!

LAOLU: Daddy! You are renouncing Jesus?

TEMMY: He is our Lord and Saviour. He died for us. He said He is coming to take us home to be with Him.

ANDERSON: Temmy, please...!

LAOLU: No, Daddy! You have taught us all these. You have preached it that we should stand in Jesus whatever happens.

OFFICER: (*to Temmy*) So, you his children have chosen the path of stubbornness also?

ANDERSON: No, Officer, please, don't listen to them.

TEMMY: Dad, Mum we heard Mummy defending her faith.

Jesus Christ is our Lord and Saviour too.

LAOLU: And He is coming to take us home

OFFICER: Now that you've made our job easier. How about you going home to meet Him over there? *(Pointing his gun to Temmy)*

ANDERSON: *(begging)* Ah! No! No! Officer! Please!
OFFICER: Tell me well to your Jesus when you see Him.

(He s shoots both one after the other. Anderson rushes to them as they are gasping a for their last breath)

ANDERSON: *(screams aloud)* Yeeh! Oh my God! Oh! Temmy! Laolu! Ah! (Simon bursts into tears at the Corner where he crouches in fear.)*

SIMON: Oh! God!

OFFICER: *(yells at Simon)* Shut your damn mouth! Have you made your own confession?

SIMON: *(fearfully)* Yes, sir...yes, sir...! I did! *(Man 1 comes back into the living room from searching all the rooms)*

MAN I: He made his own renunciation three days ago.

OFFICER: You will need to do it again before me here.

SIMON: Yes, Sir.

OFFICER: Do the renunciation now!

SIMON: (*shivering in fear*) Yes, sir.....................Jesus Christ, I Renounce You
today, as my....

OFFICER: How long have you been following your faith?

SIMON: This year is the fourteenth year, sir.

OFFICER: Fourteenth year of following your Jesus Christ and you could still deny Him after Fourteen Years? Do you know what?

SIMON: (*tensely stammers*) No..Sir! No, sir.

OFFICER: You are not trustworthy...! You can't be trusted!

SIMON: (*begging nervously*) No.! I meant everything I said with all my being! I have followed Him for Fourteen Years truly... But many times, he has not answered my prayers...I have been disappointed many times...I have waited for too long for some crucial things of life and He's yet to do them for me...! So, I have my reasons for renouncing Him now... I'm damn serious...!

OFFICER: (*yells at him*) Stand on your feet!

SIMON: Sir?

MAN II: He says get up! (*Simon quickly springs up on his feet*)

OFFICER: You are a bad follower. If I were your Jesus, I would deny you too. You cannot be trusted.

(*He points his pistol at him and fires. Simon falls backward and his body hits the floor with a thud. He coils in pain briefly before becoming motionless. Anderson looks in shock)*

OFFICER: Now, it's your turn!

Scene Three

(*Back in the uncompleted building where the family of Kenny and Tobi were hiding. The bodies of Kenny, Tobi and their youngest child, Lanre, are lying on the floor in the puddle of their own blood. Esther and Kola are tied to stakes tied together backing each other with bruises and wounds all over their bodies. Their faces are soaked in tears and bloodstains. Two men in military camouflage stand over the dead bodies. Noises of people and intermittent gunshots with periodic screams filled the night.*)

MAN I: (*standing before the children*) Your parents and your brother have died for their stubborn resolute minds. Your brother would have lived if he had not listened to the persuasion of his arrogant father. But you can live and still enjoy your lives.

ESTHER: We do not desire to live...for there is no live to enjoy when Jesus Christ is taken away from it.

MAN I: We need to end this session once and for all. We will have to take your confession immediately and end this long session.

(*He brings out the piece of paper and unfold it and begin to read.*)

MAN I: You, first. Please, say this after me – Jesus Christ..

ESTHER: (*Crying*) Jesus Christ...
MAN I: I..

ESTHER: (*cuts in*) Excuse me, Officer. May I ask you one question?

MAN I: I am sorry, we must end this long session. We have been here longer than necessary.

ESTHER: I and my brother here will die today. Because we will not renounce Jesus Christ. We are eager to go and meet our parents. They are waiting at the other side for us.

MAN I: Other side, where?

KOLA: In heaven...they are in heaven now. We want to go and meet them.

MAN I: Do you want to die today?

ESTHER: We are going home today, any moment from now. But if you die today, you are not coming to Heaven at all...

MAN II: You are chip of the old block. You earned your haughtiness from your parents. Are you not afraid to die?

ESTHER: Rather, I am more afraid to stay here where the peace and joy are afraid to dwell. I want to go home where the Prince of Peace dwell. Where their day never go dusk and their joy never ends.

KOLA: (*cries painfully*) Esther....! My chest is hurting. Oh! Jesus!

ESTHER: (*to the men*) When are you going to put an end to this long discuss?

MAN I: When you are ready to make a useful Confession.

ESTHER: (*tiredly*) We have already made our confessions, Sir. We choose to follow Jesus Christ till death.

(*Man I comes to her front, and points his gun at her. Esther closes her eyes as tears stream down her face*)

MAN I: Then, tell me well to Him when you see Him. Tell Him if truly He exists, I wish to see Him one day and engage Him in a useful conversation.

ESTHER: (*with her eyes still closed. She responds in low voice*) I will deliver your message.., Sir.
(*The Man stands there pointing the gun at her*)

Scene Four

(A young man is being tortured by a group of four security personnel in uniform. The man's undershirt is drenched in blood as he is pinned down on the floor by two men. One of the men holds a plier with which he pulls out the nail of his forefinger. The tortured man screams in agony, struggling on the blood-stained floor. The fourth man sitting in a chair with crossed legs seems to be a senior officer.)

OFFICER COLLINS: *(asking the tortured man)* We removed only the nail of one finger out of ten. And we shall remove the nails one after the other until all the tears in your eyes are exhausted and there are no tears anymore to shed.

TORTURED MAN: *(groaning aloud)*
Ah-a-a-a! Noooo! Ple-e-e-e-ase!

OFFICER COLLINS: Then, answer my question:

TORTURED MAN: Ah! Plea-a-a-a-se!

OFFICER COLLINS: Ever before we sent to fish you out, we already knew you and gathered our information about you. But you

must tell us everything about yourself, then, we shall consider if we are to be lenient with you or not.

TORTURED MAN: Ah! Please-e-e-e! I will talk, sir. I will say everything, sir.

OFFICER COLLINS: (*brings out a piece of paper and begin to look and read it up*) You are Marvellous Hezokwat. You are from East Africa. You came into this country three years ago. You are the choir master of The Cherith Pentecostals. You have waxed 9 Christian song albums and you were on invitation to sing at Annual Concert of the Downtown Christian Church when our men stormed the place you were all hiding. Yes, or no?

TORTURED MAN: (*groaning*) Ah! Yes...Yes...Sir.

OFFICER COLLINS: We have captured the rest of your co-rebels, but you would need to answer the critical questions again: Who is Jesus Christ to you?

TORTURED MAN: I have said it...Sir...I said it...

OFFICER COLLINS: You said the wrong answer, it cost you a nail from your fingers. Another wrong answer would pull off the nail from another finger. Who is Jesus Christ to you?

TORTURED MAN: I have sung about him several times. I have told you who He is to me. (*A long whip land on his back violently. He coils with pain and screams very loud*)

OFFICER COLLINS: (*shouts aloud*) Who is Jesus Christ? Answer my Question!

TORTURED MAN: (*shouts back in pain and defiance*) He is the Son of the Most High God!

(*Another whip lands on his blood-soaked bare back*)

TORTURED MAN: He is the King of kings and Lord of lords.

(Another loud harsh whip on his back makes him groans painfully)

TORTURED MAN: He is coming back to take us home to Heaven.

(They land another hard lash on his back again. He Screams)
TORTURED MAN: By Him, all things were created, visible and invisible...dominion, power and all authorities...

OFFICER COLLINS: *(angrily)* Stop!

TORTURED MAN: For God so love the world that He gave His only begotten son, that whosoever believes in Him should not perish but have everlasting live! Do you believe this, Sir?

OFFICER COLLINS: *(springs up to his feet. He orders his men)* Bring him up on his feet. Let him stand up! *(The men pull him up and hold him while the Senior Officer boils in rage)* Shut the hell up!

(He brings out a short gun from his thigh and point it to his head)

TORTURED MAN: *(standing wobbly in between the two men in groans and pains)* Jesus Christ, forgive me all my sins...and receive my Soul... Please, Jesus...Have mercy on me...!

SENIOR OFFICER: *(roars hotly)* now, for the last time, who is Jesus to You?

(The tortured man stands straight on his painful legs, makes a military salute with his hand up on the side of his face and begins to sing)

I have heard how Christians long ago Were brought before a tyrants throne. And they were told that he would spare their lives If they would renounce the name of Christ. But one by one they chose to die The Son of God they would not deny Like a great angelic choir sings I can almost hear their voices ring:

I pledge allegiance to the Lamb With all my strength, With all I am

I will seek to honor His commands I pledge allegiance to the
Lamb

The Son of God...
My Saviour and my Redeemer...! The Lord of the....

*(The Officer pulls the trigger and shoots him at close range. The
man falls backward and hits the floor as blood oozes out of the
bullet hole).*

Scene Five

(Inside a large church. A group of worshippers numbering about twenty-five are gathering in fear. Apprehension is boldly manifesting on their faces some are crying and trembling. The doors of the church are locked up. And Pastor Larry stands before them admonishing them and encouraging them.)

PASTOR LARRY: *(cautiously speaking in low voice)* Brethren, calm down and listen to the Word of the Lord from the Book of Isaiah 43:2. He says concerning us: "When you pass through the waters, I wvill be with you; And through the rivers, they shall not overflow you. When you walk through the fire, you shall not be burned, Nor shall the flame scorch you". Brother Alex, Mummy Rowland, relax. The Lord is with us like a Might One in Battle. He will defend us.

BROTHER ALEX: *(panicking and shivering)* Pastor Sir. Ah! My wife and children...I don't know where they ran to. I thought they were following me when we were running towards the church. I got to the doorway of the church and looked back. I could not find them. Ah! God!

(There is a loud desperate banging on the door of the church)

MUMMY ROWLAND: There is someone at the door.

ALEX: (*panicky*) Ah! It's my wife and children! Ah! They must be my wife and children! Pastor, Praise God. They have come.

(*Going to open the door as the banging of the door continues*)

PASTOR LARRY: Bro Alex... What if they are not the ones knocking the door?

ALEX: Pastor, what if they are the ones knocking the door, and they are presently at risk standing outside?

(*He moves to the door as the rest people hasten to hide anywhere. He gets to the door, unlocks the door and removes the bar behind the door. He cautiously opens the door to look outside. The door is pushed in and a lady rushes inside and shuts the door back again and bars it.*)

THE LADY: (*apprehensively*) Ah..Daddy, Sir. Pastor, please help me.....! Help me...!

PASTOR: What happened? Who are you?

THE LADY: The Black Eagles...! They are coming after me...!

(*The people begin to panic and move around to hide.*)

MUMMY ROWLAND: You this lady, they are coming after you and you ran here...you are leading them to this place to find us...

THE LADY: (*apprehensively*) No-o! Pastor, I never knew there were people here. I wanted to open the door and storm inside here to hide, but I met the door locked. That is why I was banging the door....

PASTOR: (*Displeased*) Lady what have you done? You shouldn't have come towards here.

THE LADY: Where else should I have run to? I thought the church is a refuge place. This was where I was converted two months ago, Pastor, and I have attended the discipleship class of this church. I am a young Christian, but I was taught here about following Jesus Christ and loving Him. How come you now reject me in the face of persecutions?

A MAN: (*angrily*) You are not wise at all! The Black Eagles are pursuing you and you were leading them towards this place! Do you want to endanger our lives? Even if you are a young Christian, shouldn't you be wise?

(*Sound of Police siren begins to approach the place. They are scared. Shortly, the siren light flickers into the church and the people become frightened and trembling, looking for hiding places. The door of the*

main entrance is burst opened as a man in black uniform and red bandana head scarf walks inside. He is followed by three other uniformed gunmen.)

THE OFFICER: Eh! Pastor, we are not here to waste time. Time is not on our side. Gather all your people here. Let them all come out of their hiding-places, and don't let me search them out.

PASTOR: (*stammers*) We are...all here. No one is hiding anywhere.

THE OFFICER: Pastor, I warned you. Call all your people to gather here and don't give me any stress.

PASTOR: (*calls aloud*) Please, everyone, wherever you are, come out here.

THE OFFICER: If I search the whole place, whoever we find hiding shall be shot dead immediately without any question or chance to speak. Call them out here.

PASTOR: (*nervously*) Everyone, come out here!

(*They all begin to walk out of the corners and gather in front of the altar, shaking and trembling in fear.*)

THE OFFICER: Reverend, as you are aware, we are ordered to establish the New Order. You are either here or there. We do not want the Jesus Fanatics in our midst anymore.

Therefore, we are getting rid of all those who are standing for Jesus and sparing those who are renouncing Him. Do I make myself clear?

THE PEOPLE: (*shaking in fear, and some already sobbing*)
Yes...Sir!

THE OFFICER: (*turns to the Pastor*) I suppose you should lay a very good example for your flock. And you may choose to lay a very bad one. You ought to have trained them to follow their Leader. So, I am starting from you, Reverend. Are you for Jesus or against Him? Would you Confess Him or Deny Him?

(The Pastor pauses. Looking at the congregated people, opens his mouth to speak, but pauses again. The Lady steps forward.)

THE LADY: Pastor, two months ago. I gave my life to Jesus Christ here in this church. I came out for the Altar Call, and I knelt here at this spot to accept Jesus as my Lord and Saviour. You have taught us to be ready to stand for our faith in the face of persecutions in office and campus.

THE OFFICER: Young Lady, it's not yet your turn. I want the Reverend to lead his flock. So, keep your mouth shut. *(Turns to the Pastor)* Reverend, I call you today to make a single decision for all your congregation here. I would not ask any question from any of them. I would ask you and you would decide for them. Is that a deal?

(Pastor remains speechless as his open mouth in hesitation to talk)

THE OFFICER: Reverend, say something on behalf of your People! Are you for Jesus Christ or against Him? You stand for Him, and all of you would be killed within five minutes. And if you decide to renounce Him, all of you would be released to go home. What do you say, Reverend?

(Hesitantly, he opens his mouth again with shaking lips.)

THE OFFICER: Reverend, why is it taking this long for you to decide? Are you standing for Jesus or against Him? Speak for your people!

(He glances at the people who are looking confused and some begging him to spare their lives, while some are just kneeling in tears and silent prayers. The Lady steps out again.)

THE LADY: Officer, can I speak for rest of us?

THE OFFICER: I guess so, young lady.

THE LADY: Our Pastor had already told us that Jesus Said, in His father's house are many mansions. So, if all of us die tonight, there are mansions to occupy all of us!

A MAN: (shouts suddenly) Nooo! I hope you are not crazy! I just think you are not insane! Are you alright? You and who are

going to occupy a stupid mansion in Heaven? Have you been to heaven and verified if there is any Mansion in Heaven for you? Officer, sir.

THE OFFICER: Yes.

MAN: I will speak for myself, sir. Others can speak for themselves. They said Jesus is coming back again, how are we sure he is coming back again. They have been giving us this century- long promise and He has not still come. So, that promise is a lie. Officer sir, Me I don't believe in Jesus Christ, I have been a member of this church just for social and business connections. Nothing more. I don't have Jesus in my life, in the first place, so there is nothing to deny or renounce. I don't believe in Him.

THE OFFICER: Step aside, then.
(The man steps aside from the other group.)

THE OFFICER: In that case, you have made the work easier for us. Those of you who belong to Jesus be on the side of this Lady. And let the others who don't believe in Him as their Lord be on the side of this man.

(Quietly and slowly, people begin to move one after the other. Six people move to the side of the Lady, while the rest fifteen people move to the side of the man. The Pastor remains on the spot without moving.)

THE OFFICER: Reverend, on which part are you? All those who are standing on the side of this Lady tonight are going to die, by the order of the authority from above. So, where do you belong?

(He remains without moving, looking at the people hesitantly.

THE OFFICER: Reverend, are you ashamed to make your choice? If you believe Jesus is your Lord, then move to His side. And if not, move to the other side and let us know where you belong.

(The Officer points his gun at him in anger)

THE OFFICER: Enough of this display of childishness. I will count to five, and if you don't make your choice, I will kill you before these people. Move to where you belong! One....!Two... Three...!

(Slowly, to the amazement of some of them, the Pastor comes down from the altar and walks to the side of the Man.)

THE LADY: (*in shock*) Ah! Pastor, do you know what you are doing?

You denied Jesus?

PASTOR: No, Dearest Sister, on the contrary. He who runs from a fight, lives to fight another day.

THE LADY: From what Book of the Bible is that?

PASTOR: From the Elders Book of Wisdom.

THE LADY: (*astonished*) Is that in the Bible?

MUMMY ROWLAND: (*shocked*) Pastor, I am surprised you are afraid to die for the Lord?

PASTOR: No, on the contrary, Mrs. Rowland. Wisdom is profitable to direct.

THE OFFICER: Enough! You have made your choices, so be it!

THE LADY: (*speaks loudly with astonishment*) Pastor, you preached to us that Jesus Loves us and we should love Him in return, but here, in the face of persecution, you denied Him! You denied Jesus, Pastor!

(*The Officer dips his hand into his breast pocket and brings out a whistle. He blows it loudly, and the entrance door opens. Two men in red overall uniform walk inside each of them, carrying a workbox. They get to the people standing behind the man.*)

OFFICER: We shall give you CFI. Your Classified Freedom Identification. This is the mark of the New Order and with this, you are not a threat to the sanctity of the populace. You are free to move anywhere without any harassment from the New Order Security Force.

(The two men open the red boxes and brings out the instrument of the CFI, looking like an infrared thermostat. They apply it on their foreheads and the mark is like a round red patch on their forehead. When the CFI marking is completed, the two men closed the boxes and carry it and walk out of the church again)

THE OFFICER: Now, all of you standing for Jesus, file out into the bus outside the building, to the execution centre. Move!

(All the seven people line up in tears and apprehension as a man leads them, and another man guides them as they flee out of the church building into the bus positioned outside the church. All the security officers and gunmen enter the bus and the drive off. Inside the Church, the Pastor and the rest people are still apprehensive and nervous. A man hastens to the window to peep outside, and rushes back to the gathering)

THE MAN: They have gone... Ah! They have taken them to execution place.

(Outside, two men arrive on motorbikes, dismount, and rush into the church, bursting open the main entrance door. The gathered people are scared again, as they all try to pack themselves behind the Pastor. The two men are hiding their eyes behind a bandana mask that covers only the portion of eyes above their nose)

MAN I: Some people are hiding inside this Church!

MAN II: Ah-aah! Pastor Larry! Are these your people? PASTOR: Yes, these are my people, and we have all made our choice.

MAN I: I can see it by the CFI mark on your forehead. So, you've made your choices.

THE PEOPLE: (*nervously*) Yes...Yes...Sir...

(*They remove their eyes masks, and their eyes and faces can now be well seen*)

PASTOR: (*shocked*) Ah! These faces are very familiar to me! Have we met before?

MAN I: Your memory served you well, Pastor. We have been in this church before, and you preached, and we came out for the Altar Call for salvation. We attended this church for more than one year while you taught us many things about God and Heaven.

PASTOR: Ah!

MAN I: It shocked you? We knew it! That you are fake! Pastor Larry, you are a bunch of hypocrites! You were teaching us what you never believed in! You taught us to follow Jesus and stand with him till the end, but you never have the gut stand for Him.

MAN II: When you were teaching all those studies, what was in your mind? To deceive your congregation and push them to death while you stay chicken away and stay alive. Majority of your congregation have been killed for defending their faith, here you are with the CFI mark.

MAN I: We have been running and hiding, and when we wanted to come into the Church and join you people, we sighted the car of the New Order Police coming towards this church, so we hid ourselves and was watching from nearby uncompleted building.

MAN II: We were shocked that you were not among those they filed up and conveyed to the special execution ground. As they were entering the bus, we noticed you were not among those arrested. We knew you have compromised. You have agreed to receive the CFI mark.

MAN I: You disappointed us, Pastor.

MAN II: You denied the Jesus you have preached about all these years?

PASTOR: (*stammers*) Yes...he who runs from fight lives to fight another day.

MAN II: (*wonders*) Pastor, you denied your Jesus? And how are you sure you would live to fight another day?

PASTOR: (*fearfully, inaudibly*) ...Actually...

(*Man, I bring out a gun from his side pocket. It's a pistol. He points the gun at him in anger as he trembles, and the rest of the people run back from him*)

MAN I: You betrayed...your Master...!

PASTOR: (*scared*) What are you trying to do?

MAN I: Trying to do the needful.

PASTOR: (*shaking*) No! you can't kill me.

MAN I: Says who?

MAN I: Die the death of Judas...!

(He pulls the trigger at close range, and the loud sound of the bullet throws his body backward on the ground. He dies instantly, the rest people are shocked, running to different area.)

MAN I: *(disgusted)* You are disgusting, Pastor! Your type is nauseating! You are worst that Judas!

(He spits on his body disdainfully and the men walk out of the church, mount the motorbikes again and zoom off)

Scene Six

(Same night. The bus travels through some bushes and hidden paths, and then arrive in front of a warehouse. It stops and all the uniformed men get down from the bus and two of them stand by the door mouth of the bus, holding their guns.)

GUNMAN I: All right; get down very quick and walk into the death chamber.

(They people begin to disembark in fear and trembling; shivering in tears as they line up in a single file.)

THE LADY: *(tearfully)* King of Glory...! I am coming over, Jesus! I want to close my eyes and wake up in the Land of Glory, Jesus!

GUNMAN II: Come on, Move! Move!

(They are lined up in single file. Infrequent gunshots, screams and shouting of many people are coming forth from inside the warehouse. A young woman runs out of the line and attempts to

running away as two of the security officers run after her and holds her down)

OFFICER I: *(holding her)* Where do you think you are going? You have made your decisions.

YOUNG WOMAN: (*screaming*) Nooo! I am not going in there! I change my mind! I change my confession! Please-e-e!

OFFICER I: No, you can't change your mind here..

(*A deep voice of a Senior Officer roars from the entrance door of the Chamber*)

OFFICER COLLINS: And why not?

OFFICER: Commander told us no one can change his mind here.

OFFICER COLLINS: Commander told us to use our discretion. Bring her here. (*The two officers pull her to the Senior Officer, drenched in tears and trembling*) What?

YOUNG WOMAN: (*shivering in fears*) Please, I want to change my mind...!

OFFICER COLLINS: And why?

YOUNG WOMAN: I don't want to die now...Please... ! I choose to live.

OFFICER COLLINS: You can't change your mind outside the chamber here. You will do so inside the chamber when you stand before the stake.

YOUNG WOMAN: (*pleading*) No.! Please...! I can feel the smell of death already...Don't let me go inside the Chamber.

AN ELDERLY MAN: (*shouts aloud at her*) Woman, why are you fearing death and you want to deny the Lord your Saviour? Are you not happy dying as martyr? Closing your eyes here and opening them in the land of bliss and splendour... where you never again live in pains and agony. Where all worries are past, and troubles are gone? Don't deny Him...who cast aside His glory to secure for you free salvation from eternal agony.

OFFICER COLLINS: Now, join the line and go inside. All of you!

(*They are entering into the chamber as the screams and shouts are mixed with the sporadic rattling of gunshots*)

Scene Seven

(It is a large hall in shape of a big warehouse. Some dead bodies litter the ground in blood. Some security men are carrying out some bodies into a waiting truck outside. A little bit far before them, some six people are tied to stakes, while some security men are positioned before them with guns to execute them. The people tied to the stakes are three men and two ladies. The people who just entered now are made to sit on the floor, in terrible fear, at a corner looking at the execution spot.)

OFFICER COLLINS: *(to the gunmen)* Take your positions!

(The gunmen aim their guns at the people tied to stakes)

OFFICER COLLINS: Pastors and Preachers, I want to ask you for the last time if you wish to change your mind and choose to live.

(In unison, the voices of the people ring out with smiling faces that are focused on life after the gunfire. They begin to sing)

ALL: *(begin to sing with smiles and tears on their faces)*
1.   *Si o Olutunu Orun Fun ore at'agbara Re Si O,*
        ife eni t'Owa Ninu Majemu Olorun A nko, Aleluya

2.	*Si O agbara Eni ti*
	O nwe ni mO, t'o nWO ni san A nko, Aleluya

(When they finish the song, they stand in reverence salute as the Senior Officer shouts his order)

OFFICER COLLINS: *(to the Gunmen)* Fire..!

(The Gunmen open a rain of bullets on them as their bodies vibrate till, they become motionless.)

Scene Eight

(A truck full of New Order police has arrived the front of the compound of a notable minister of God. The gunmen rush down from the truck and badge into the main door of the compound. They are confronted by three men who armed with cutlass, gun, and axe. The gunmen point their guns at them and give them orders)

COMMANDER: What is the meaning of this? You confronting us with arms? Is this what your Reverend has ordered you to do? He has ordered you all to defend yourselves.

MAN I: *(holding up his cutlass defiantly)* I stand against you in the name of the Lord of Host. You came against us with guns and bullet, and we stand against you in the name of the Lord of Host whom you have defied.

COMMANDER: *(calmly)* What type of childish display is this? All of you drop your weapons gently and calm down.

MAN II: *(pointing his gun at him)* No! We are acting under instructions to stand against you blood-thirsty fanatics. We

are not to allow you access into the house. We shall defend our faith.

COMMANDER: We are here to ask you simple questions and your answers would determine our actions. Now put down your weapons and answer the questions.

MAN III: No! we shall not answer any questions from you, and you are just to turn around and get out of this compound.

COMMANDER: We are acting under instructions from the higher authority. You shall answer our questions or pay dearly for your arrogance. We have come to question the Reverend too.

MAN I: You cannot get to the Reverend.

COMMANDER: Do you believe Jesus Christ as your Lord and Saviour? Just answer the simple question.

MAN II: (*waving his weapon menacingly*) It is not in your power to ask us that question.

COMMANDER: The government must ascertain where you belong.
Is Jesus the Son of God?

MAN III: We will not honour that ignoble Question with an admirable answer.

COMMANDER: We will make it easier for you. I will count to five. And we shall judge you ourselves. If you all believe Jesus is the Son of God and you have accepted him as your Lord and Saviour, put down your arms.

(Their weapons remain raised up defiantly)

COMMANDER: May I repeat myself? If you believe Jesus is the Son of God and He is coming back, as you have always claimed, to take you home in Heaven, drop your weapons.

(They glance at one another hesitantly, with their weapons now getting softer in their hands)

MAN II: And what happens to us when we drop the weapons.

COMMANDER: If you don't drop the weapons, it means you don't believe Jesus is the Son of God, and you have not accepted Him as your Lord and Saviour. If you believe in Jesus, as Your Saviour, then, drop your weapon!

MAN I: *(still pointing his gun)* No one is dropping any weapon here!

MAN II: *(lowering his Cutlass and getting nervous)* I gave my life to Christ five years ago and I have been attending this Church. I believe Jesus is the Son of God and He has forgiven me all my sins...And He is coming back to take me home to Heaven.

COMMANDER: Or you going to Heaven to meet Him. It still mean the same thing, Either He comes to you, or you go to meet Him.

MAN II: *(nervously)* Please, don't kill me!

COMMANDER: We are under instructions to kill all believers in

Jesus
Christ. Unfortunately, you must die unless you deny Him.

MAN II: (*trembling*) No...No...I can't. I can't deny He is the Son of God...I can't deny He is coming back to take me home to live with Him forever! I can't deny Him now...! Please...don't kill me...I can't deny Him...

COMMANDER: (*points his gun at him*) Then, Go and meet Him!

(*He pulls the trigger and fires. The force of the bullet throws his head backward. He hit the floor dead. The other men tremble with their weapons still raised*)

COMMANDER: We are under instructions to wipe out all those who still believe in the Jesus Christ. You heard the instructions, didn't you?

MAN I: (*they quickly lift up their weapons higher above their head in obedience*) Yes, Sir...Yes, Sir...We are at your command, Sir.

MAN II: (*trembling*) We are not ready to die, sir.

COMMANDER: Is your Reverend at home?

MAN I: Yes...Sir. He is at home...Sir.

COMMANDER: Put down all your weapons and follow us.

(*Quietly, they put down the weapons and follow the Gunmen into the house.*)

Scene Nine

(Inside a large living room, prestigiously decorated and beautifully set out. A man stands by the electronic cabinet, looking apprehensively. About eight armed men are standing in strategic positions around him. As the Gunmen walk inside, the armed men take positions and aim their guns at the men that walk inside. They gaze at each other)

COMMANDER: (*smiles calmly*) Reverend Godsman. I am Commander Effiong. The Commanding Officer in charge of the New Order Security Forces of this entire city. I needed to introduce myself to you in case you need to know it. This is surprising indeed. What nonsense is this that you are doing?

REVEREND: (*harshly*) Commander Effiong, God has not given me the spirit of fear, but of boldness and of sound mind. You think you can storm into my house and intimidate me anyhow?

COMMANDER: Was that why you have armed your men? I thought you have your Jesus Christ who can defend you. I thought He said in the Book of Matthew 5:39, that you resist not an

evil person, and whoever slaps you on the right cheek, you should turn the left side...How come you now choose to disregard His

Word and fight for your enemies.

REVEREND: (*harshly*) Because he says in Luke 22:36 "But now, he who has no sword, let him sell his garment and buy one.

COMMANDER: (*smiles faintly*) So how much did all your swords cost you? You taught your congregation to trust in the Lord and die for Jesus, while you are here surrounding yourselves with bodyguards to fight for you. Your hypocrisy stinks! Anyways, I am not here to judge you, I am here to take your confession. Tell your men to drop their weapons, we come in peace.

REVEREND: (*hotly*) If you come in peace, you would not storm into my house with guns and shoot my guards. These men are trained men and are perfect in their use of weapons. Tell your men to turn back and go out of my house.

COMMANDER: Reverend, our question is simple? We don't want to assume that you are standing for your Jesus Christ. We need to ask you by due protocols. Are you for Jesus or against Jesus?

REVEREND: (*begins to soften*) Commander,...

COMMANDER: Tell your men to drop their weapons...It is an insult pointing guns at me and my boys.

REVEREND: (*to his men*) Everyone, stand down...stand down...! (They all relax and lower their arms) Commander, I plead with you. I know what is happening. I know of the new government's directive to wipe off all believers in Jesus Christ. But I plead with you to secure my life and my family and my men here.

COMMANDER: How can that be possible, Reverend?

REVEREND: (*restlessly*) Ask me no questions. Ask us no Questions...Move on.

COMMANDER: Will that be possible?

REVEREND: In this circumstance, what is not possible does not exist.

(*Commander pauses and thinks for a while*)

COMMANDER: All right. Let's do it this way. I need to follow due process for the records. Between me and you, we would need to ask you and your men the questions.

REVEREND: Let me have the questionnaire.

COMMANDER: Reverend, do you Accept Jesus Christ as your Lord and Saviour or not? It is a simple question.

REVEREND: What if I said "Yes." What happens?

COMMANDER: If you say "Yes!" you die. But if you say "No", you live. It's the rule.

REVEREND: (*pleading softly*) But I don't want to Die, Commander.

COMMANDER: Then, say "No!".

REVEREND: Ah...! Please, Commander, don't let me say "No!"

COMMANDER: Then say "Yes!"
(*Reverend stands looking hesitantly at Commander, unable to decide*)

REVEREND: It is somehow… difficult.

COMMANDER: Reverend, do you believe Jesus Christ as your Lord and Saviour?

REVEREND: Commander, why are you doing this? Why are you putting me on edge?

COMMANDER: Reverend, answer the simple question. It is a question of "Yes" or "No".

REVEREND: And it is an answer of Death or Life.

COMMANDER: And I never knew you would be afraid to defend or deny your faith in the Jesus Christ you have preached all these years.

(*The Commander turns to the four guards surrounding Reverend.*)

COMMANDER: Can you do me a favour, Reverend?

REVEREND: What do you want me to do?

COMMANDER: Please, call all your guards inside here, every one of them. Whatever decision you make for them stands.

REVEREND: (*turns to one of the Guards*) Gather the boys here for me.

GUARD: Yes, sir. (*He dashes out immediately*)

COMMANDER: The whole process is taking longer time than necessary. When they come here, you make a single decision on behalf of them all, and that will be all. We shall be on our Way. (*The Guards all walk inside*)

REVEREND: Eh, Guys, they come in peace. Stand down all of you.

COMMANDER: You all know what is going on, there is a New Order in place. All Christians who believe in the Lord Jesus Christ are being removed to cleanse the land of fanatics and religious bigots. For the peace of everyone. But we understand, this is a church setting, and we all know what you believe in. But just to update our thinking? I would like to put forth this simple test and then, the Reverend would speak on behalf of all of you.

REVEREND: (*getting worried*) Commander, what Test are you putting forth?

COMMANDER: (*to the guards*) If you accept the Lord Jesus Christ as your Lord and saviour, stay with the Reverend. If you have nothing to do with Jesus Christ, stay here with me.

REVEREND: Commander Effiong, what are you doing?

COMMANDER: It is a simple test. If you are for Jesus, go to the Reverend's side. If you are against Jesus Christ, come here by my side.

(The Guards begin to move in the two directions. Four Guards go to the Reverend's side, and five walk to the side of Commander)

COMMANDER: Reverend, you and all these guards filling behind you have decided to take your stand for Jesus Christ as your Lord and Saviour. Is that Correct?

REVEREND: You cannot force any of us to take a position.

COMMANDER: I have done such a thing. It is a free choice. But all those who confess to stand with Jesus Christ as Christians are being wiped off. It's an order!

(He signals to the Armed Security men behind him, they point their guns to Reverend and the four guards. They are shocked.)

REVEREND: *(nervously)* Commander, hold on a bit, please.

COMMANDER: You have wasted many precious time discussing the irrelevant.

(He signals again and there is a rain of guns hots at the guards standing by the Reverend's side. The bodies drop on the ground. Reverend is still standing shaking with fear.)

REVEREND: *(shaking dreadfully)* Please Commander, spare my life.

COMMANDER: Are you for Jesus or against Jesus?

REVEREND: *(with quaking and stammering voice)* Please, I...choose to...live. I choose to...leave...!

COMMANDER: That is not the answer, Reverend.

REVEREND: Oh...! God! I am... not for Jesus.... I am not...for Jesus! I want to live...!

(A New Order Security Officer leads down the stairs the wife and two teenage children of Reverend. They come down the stairs in fright and tears. As they see dead bodies of the shot guards littering the ground, they shiek in fear.)

COMMANDER: Reverend, you lied to us that your wife and children were away, whereas you hid them in your inner rooms.

REVEREND: You never asked me of my wife and kids... Commander Effiong, please, deal gently with them.

COMMANDER: They need to answer the confession of their faith themselves.

REVEREND: I have answered for all of them...They are not dying.

COMMANDER: Rev, Mrs, the dead bodies on the floor are those who stood their ground for Jesus Christ. As you are aware of the latest development; all Christians are being wiped off to cleanse our land of their terrible fanatism and religious impunity. A stand for Jesus Christ earns you an instant death and a denial give your life.

REV. MRS: *(impatiently)* Which stupid denial will earn you nonsense life? The Bible says in John 12:25, "He who loves his life will lose it, and he who hates his life in this world will keep it for eternal life. So where did you get the idea that denying Jesus

Christ would earn your life? No, you deny Jesus Christ, you

lose your life in Eternity; only standing for Him and confessing Him can you earn an Eternal Life.

COMMANDER: Rev. Mrs, your husband just made his choice to live.

REV. MRS: He did what...? No, it is impossible. Eric, Eric...don't tell me you denied Jesus Christ in order not to die, because you just signed in for Eternal condemnation if truly you did. Tell me this officer is lying...

(Reverend stands staring speechlessly)

REV. MRS: Speak up and tell me, this is a joke, Eric! Eric! Tell me this is not true! How can you deny Jesus Christ you have been preaching about all your 35 years in ministry? No! I can't believe this! Eric...! Wake up and tell them you were joking!

(He looks on speechlessly. The woman burst into tears)

REV. MRS. Eric...! You betrayed Jesus Christ because of the fear of death! You nailed Him to the Cross the second time! Eric...! You taught us the Bible...you taught us the Biblical doctrines. You taught your congregations things about God! Eric...What happened?

COMMANDER: Madam...We need to take your confession as quickly as possible. And your teenage children too would have to speak for themselves. Do you believe in Jesus Christ

as your Lord and Saviour? A Yes" would earn you Death, but a

"No" would bring you an instant Death. What do you say?

REV. MRS: (*gathering her tearing teenage children by her side, as tears stream down their faces*) As for me and my house, we shall serve the Lord Jesus Christ. I and the children the Lord has given to me are for signs and wonders in their generation. We stand for the Lord.

COMMANDER: I am sorry, Rev. Mrs, your children are of age and should make their choices for themselves:

(*The Rev. Mrs and her children make a military salute sign with their hands to the side of their face and start singing*)

I have heard how Christians long ago Were brought before a
tyrant's throne
And they were told that he would spare their lives If they would
renounce the name of Christ
But one by one they chose to die The Son of God they would not
deny Like a great angelic choir sings
I can almost hear their voices ring

I pledge allegiance to the Lamb With all my strength, With all I
am I will seek to honor His commands I pledge allegiance to the
Lamb

COMMANDER: May I then take this for your open confession of where you stand?

(*He gives a sign to his armed officers; they raise up their gun and point the guns at them. Rev. Mrs and the Children drop on their knees reverently as the Officers open fire on them, dropping their bodies on the floor. Reverend raises up a loud sorrowful cry, wailing loudly. Commander blows his whistle, and two men walk inside in red overall suits, each carrying a kit box. The two men open the red boxes and brings out the instrument of the CFI. They apply the red patch on their foreheads. When the CFI marking is completed, the two men closed the boxes and walk out of the large living room, leaving the Reverend behind wailing)*

REVEREND: *(crying loudly)* What did I just do? Denied the Lord? Afraid of dying for Him? No…No…I am for Jesus Christ! He is my Saviour…! I want to die for Him. ………………………………………!

Scene Ten

(Inside a moderately furnished spacious living room, an elderly man in his late fifties is sitting in a chair that is positioned to face the entrance of the closed door of the living room. Beside the chair is a Bible and a glass cup of water. He sits so calmly and quietly with his legs crossed and the Bible opened on his lap. He Carries the cup of water to his mouth, sipping the water when he hears sirens of police car arriving in front of his house. He remains unperturbed as he still holds the cup of water in his hand, expecting the entrance door to open any time. Soon, there is a loud repeated bang on the doo.)

THE MAN: *(calmly)* Yes, the door is opened, you may come in.

(The main door is pushed opened and a senior officer of the New Order Security Force walks inside, followed by four armed officers)

OFFICER COLLINS: I am Lieutenant Collins, of the New Order Security Force, empowered to enforce the New Order. As you are aware, we are commissioned to cleanse our society of all these religious bigots causing confusions everywhere.

MACAULEY: *(smiles calmly)* Welcome, Oficer Collins.

OFFICER COLLINS: We've come to take your confession, Pastor

Macauley.

MACAULEY: (*unmoved*) You have kept me waiting for more than four hours?

OFFICER COLLINS: We've been to your church.

MACAULEY: I have been told you shot and killed my wife while she was standing on the altar with some other Women.

OFFICER COLLINS: She made the choice that killed her, and we are sorry, we could not help her.

MACAULEY: She has gone ahead of me to wait for me at the river.

OFFICER COLLINS: We left her body with the bodies of many of the church members in the swamp of their own blood, right inside the church. It was not at the river side.

MACAULEY: I was told there is a question I must answer before I am sent forth.

OFFICER COLLINS: (*wonders*) Are you not afraid to die?

MACAULEY: And why should I?

OFFICER COLLINS: I have come across many pastors and believers in Jesus like yourself who switched the faith and renounced the Jesus you stick your neck out for.

MACAULEY: Those pastors and Christians you met who denied the faith and switched their confessions have endangered their souls eternally. They forgot about their heavenly mansions. They forget about the marriage feast of the Lamb; they forgot about the New Jerusalem; they forget about walking on the golden streets of Heaven. They forgot about the Millennium Age, the glorious Kingdom of a thousand years in the reign of Christ, where we shall rule with Him in glory and splendour; they forgot the New Earth and the Heaven where there shall no more be seas and the present Heavens shall pass away. They forget to remember the glorious Eternal Future and they pitched their tents with everlasting agony.

OFFICER COLLINS: All those things you mentioned, are they real?

MACAULEY: Officer Collins, Are you real?

OFFICER COLLINS: You are seeing me standing and you are asking me? Of Course, I am.

MACAULEY: Yes, everything I said about those places I said, are more real than you are. Officer Collins, may I ask you a question?

OFFICER COLLINS: I am the one to ask you a question of life and death here.

MACAULEY: Yes, what if that is my last wish before you ask me the question of life and death. I humbly request.

OFFICER COLLINS: OK. I proudly accept. You may go ahead with your last wish. Ask your question.

MACAULEY: Officer Collins, you are surely going to die one day. And after you die, what next? Where will you be after you die? There are two places to be: Heaven or Hell fire. Which is your eternal destination?

OFFICER COLLINS: And you believe those illogical religious philosophies?

MACAULEY: Is it an illogical philosophy that every offender must be punished for their sins and all criminals, after due process of the law must either be found innocent and set free of found guilty and sentenced to jail?

OFFICER COLLINS: That is not an illogical philosophy, which is normal analytical civil regulation.

MACAULEY: And I am telling you a very authentic spiritual fact, that all men have sinned and come short of the glory of God, and all men have been sentenced to eternal death in Hell Fire, as

everlasting punishment and there is a way of escape for anyone who wants to be forgiven of their sins.

OFFICER COLLINS: I am not interested in your gibberish. I am not in the....

(One of the four Guards who came inside with him responds)

GUARD: *(stammers nervously)* I am...interested, sir...

(Shocked. They all look in his direction with astonishment. Officer Collins stares at him unbelievably)

OFFICER COLLINS: Excuse me...You said something. ?
*(The Guard, shaking with fear, lowers his gun and slowly lays it

down)

OFFICER COLLINS: You said something now, what was it..?

GUARD: My Mum...was a believer. in Jesus Christ before she was felled by the bullets of the Security Forces, for her unwavering faith...She used to tell us all these. Pastor Macauley is right..I am interested in the way of escape, sir...

OFFICER COLLINS: (*stunned*) Corporal Gary, do you really know the implication of what you just said?

GUARD: (*nervously*) Absolutely., sir. I want to change. I want to go back. to where I belonged, Sir.

OFFICER COLLINS: At the Headquarters, during your enlistment into the New Order Guards, you all made a confession of oath to stand on the side of the Government to flush out all the Jesus fanatics.

GUARD: (*drops on his knees*) I have killed too many people, sir...I have shed the blood of those who stood for Jesus Christ that my Mum had preached to me severally which I had stubbornly refused. Now I saw how some people were standing for that Jesus Christ and how many people were denying Him to live. But I want to stand on the side of
Jesus Christ.., Sir.

OFFICER COLLINS: I need to get your point right, Corporal Gary. Are you saying you now stand for Jesus Christ as your Lord and Saviour?

GARY: (*with low voice*) Yes, Sir.

OFFICER COLLINS: (*loudly*) That Jesus Christ is now Your Lord and Saviour? Talk to me very loudly!

GARY: (*shouts aloud, militarily*) Yes, Sir!

OFFICER COLLINS: That you are standing for Jesus?

GARY: (*affirmatively loud*) Sir, yes, Sir.

(*Then, he pulls out a pistol from his side pocket, points it to the Guard at close range*)

OFFICER COLLINS: (**shouts loudly**) Who is Jesus Christ to you?

GARY: (*with shaking voice and teary eyes*) My Lord!... My Saviour! Jesus, save my soul! Heal.. my heart! My Saviour, forgive me all my sins and write my name in your Book of the Living. I accept you into my heart and....

(*Officer Collins fires at him at close range, the bullet flings him back unto the ground as blood oozes from the bullet hole of his head., streaming on the ground where his body lies motionless*)

OFFICER COLLINS: Now, enough of time wasting. Pastor Macauley, all protocols observed, we need to take your confessional statement.

(*He begins to sing with a smile on his face*)

MACAULEY: (sings)

*Shall we gather at the river? Where bright angel feet have trod
With its crystal tide forever Flowing by the throne of God*

*Yes, we'll gather at the river
The beautiful, the beautiful river*

Gather with the saints at the river That flows by the throne of God

*Ere we reach the shining river, Lay we every burden down; Grace
our spirits will deliver, And provide a robe and crown.*

*Yes, we ll gather at the river
The beautiful, the beautiful river Gather with the saints at the river
That flows by the throne of God*

*Soon we'll reach the shining river Soon our pilgrimage will cease
Soon our happy hearts will quiver With the melody of peace*

*Yes, we'll gather at the river
The beautiful, the beautiful river Gather with the saints at the....*

*(Officer Collins raises his gun at Pastor Macauley and fires. The
Pastor sinks in his chair as blood oozes from his chest)*

OFFICER COLLINS: (*angrily*) Get the hell out of here and go and
drown in your fantasy river.

(He turns to his guards and other security officers)

OFFICER COLLINS: We move.

*(His guards follow him as he walks out of the house into the waiting
Security Patrol jeep outside.*

Scene Eleven

(Officer Collins sits tiredly in a chair inside a roughly arranged room. It is in the middle of the night, the full moon shining in the sky over his head as he sits behind a table of hot bottles of wine. And butts cigarette oozing smokes from the smouldering ends. He takes a glassful of drink and turns I over into his mouth and slams the base of the glass cup on the table before him. He squeezes the smouldering end of the cigar in his hand in the ashtray, drunk and troubled. He drops his head on his folded arm on the table. The most recent incidence of his close member of his squad, Corporal Gary, flashes across his troubled mind)

OFFICER COLLINS: *(shouts loudly)* Who is Jesus Christ to you?

GARY: *(with shaking voice and teary eyes)* My Lord!. My Saviour! Jesus, save my soul! Heal... my heart! My Saviour, forgive me all my sins and write ny name in your Book of the Living. I accept you into my heart and....

(Officer Collins fires at him at close range, the bullet flings him back unto the ground as blood oozes from the bullet hole of his head.,

streaming on the ground where his body lies motionless)
(He jerks up, breathing heavily, looking scared, as more pictures flash across his mind, giving him more emotional turbulence:

OFFICER COLLINS: Now, enough of time wasting. Pastor Macauley, all protocols observed, we need take your confessional statement.

(He begins to sing with a smile on his face)

MACAULEY: *(sings)*
Shall we gather at the river Where bright angel feet have trod
With its crystal tide forever Flowing by the throne of God
Yes, well gather at the river
The beautiful, the beautiful river Gather with the saints at the
river That flows by the throne of God

(Officer Collins raises his gun at Pastor Macauley and fires. The Pastor sinks in his chair as blood oozes from his chest)

OFFICER COLLINS: *(angrily)* Get the hell out of here and go and drown in your fantasy river.

(He jolts into consciousness again, sweating and breathing noisily. One of his squad officers' storms inside)

OFFICER COLLINS: Yes...? You bumped in without knocking?

OFFICER: Sir, Major is here

OFFICER COLLINS: Who

OFFICER: Major Lambert, sir. The Area Commander.

(As he slothfully rises on his feet, a tall dark officer walks inside hastily. Officer Collins stands in military salute)

AREA COMMANDER: Lieutenant, I do not expect you here at this time. The time now, is 3.30hrs in the morning. We have the mandate to clear our area of all Jesus Fanatics before the dot of seven in the morning. You have three more major spots to clear. A group of religious radicals are presently gathering in a secret shelter by the Tollgate. Go there now with your squad and clear off the place.

OFFICER COLLINS: (*coldly*) Yes, sir.

AREA COMMANDER: We got an instruction from the Headquarters to change our questioning tactics to speed up with time.

OFFICER COLLINS: Yes, sir.

AREA COMMANDER: No long questionings again. No wasting of time. Standing for Jesus, you die. Turning from Jesus, you live. Make everything snappy.

OFFICER COLLINS: Yes, sir.

AREA COMMANDER: Move now! The Lion Squad will go and clear the second location. The Polar Bear will handle the Jesus Heretics hiding at a Prayer Mountain along the Express Highway. Our Surveillance Drones have located all their hiding places. Let's move!

OFFICER COLLINS: Yes, sir.

(*Calls aloud at his squad*)

OFFICER COLLINS: Wild Tiger Squad, we move!

(They all move out of the space into the jeep parked outside and they drive off.)

Scene Tweleve

(The Wild Tiger Squad of Officer Collins arrive a bushy place in their jeep. They armed officers jumped down the jeep and rush down a footpath, followed by Officer Collins. They storm on a group of people who are reverently kneeling in prayers and man stands their front leading them. The men open their eyes at the noisy arrival of the armed security officers, they look unperturbed. The armed men surround them, with their guns pointing to the praying men.)

OFFICER COLLINS: Ladies and gentlemen, you all under arrest by the law of the Federation. You are all aware of the law of cleansing the land of all fanatical religious groups. Therefore, arise on your feet as we take your confession of faith according to the standing rules. You stand for Jesus, you die. You deny Him you live. You may make an individual confession, or you may stand present you're as a group. May you all stand on your feet, please.

(The people all stand on their feet quietly), looking calm and unscared)

OFFICER COLLINS: If you are standing for Jesus and are ready to die for Him, stay over there. But if you want to deny Him and live your life in peace joy, come over here to our side.

THE LEADER: *(The leader begins to sing:) Bojumo ooo!*
A Opade ooo!

Bojumo, A opade ara wa lojo kan o! Lojo kan..!

OTHERS: *(The rest pick up the Choruses in unison) Bojumo ooo!*
A Opade ooo!
B'ojumo, A opade ara wa lojo kan o! Lojo kan o!
Lojo kan...!

OTHERS: *(the people begin to sing and go round, shaking the hands of one another and hugging one another with smiles.)*

"Bojumo ooo!
A Opade ooo!
B'ojumo, A opade ara wa lojo kan o! Lojo kan o!
Lojo kan...!

OFFICE COLLINS: *(surprised)* Is there no one willing to deny Him and live?

(The singing and the handshakes and hugging continue to the amazement of the armed squad)

OFFICE COLLINS: Then, may I take this as your group confessional statement that you all stand for your faith?

(The singing continues still)

OFFICE COLLINS: And may I kindly remind you of the implications of your stand? Confess Him you die! Deny Him you live!

(He watches them as they continue to sing, shaking hands and hugging with smile)

OFFICE COLLINS: Leader of the group, we may have to treat you specially.

(Two armed men walk to the man leading the song and pull him away from the midst of the people as he continues leading the song. Officer Collins calls a loud order)

OFFICE COLLINS: Set yourselves and aim your guns. *(The armed men aim their guns as the song still goes on)*

OFFICE COLLINS: And. ....fire!

(The rain of bullets hit the singing people as they drop on the floor one after the other, sinking the sound of their song. The group Leader becomes terrified, breaks free from their hold, and tries to run out of the church. The armed men dash after him and grab him and drag him to the presence of Officer Collins who keeps looking at him with surprise.)

GROUP LEADER: *(frightened)* Oh...God! Oh...God!

OFFICER COLLINS: *(looks astonished)* Were you not displaying courage in the presence of your group members? Why the sudden change...?

GROUP LEADER: *(stammers in fright)* I. don't want to die...
OFFICER COLLINS: *(shocked)* You don't want to die?
GROUP LEADER: *(quivering)* No, Sir...I don't want to die, Sir.

OFFICER COLLINS: Why...? Why would you deny the Lord, you claimed you love at this time?

GROUP LEADER: I... I am not ready to meet Him, Sir.

OFFICER COLLINS: Not ready to meet Him? Why?

GROUP LEADER: My life is not right before Him, Sir...My whole life is full of secret sins I have not repented of, Sir...If I should die

with my colleagues,...I am sure I would not see His face... My life is dent with fornication and adultery...I lead the Praises and Worship, but my heart is soaked in dirt. Severally, I have lodged in hotel rooms with Shalley, who is the Leader of the Counselling Team. Three times she had aborted pregnancies for me to cover up our adulterous atrocities. I am dirty..and stinking! I cannot appear before Him like this...I have not prepared myself for Eternal glory..

OFFICER COLLINS: Then, deny Him and live!

GROUP LEADER: No...! I will never turn my back against him. But I don't want to die in this state of my heart. I don't want to close my eyes on earth and open them in Hell. Sir.

OFFICER COLLINS: May I take your confessional statement now?

GROUP LEADER: There is no need to. I will always love Him, and He is my Lord and Master.

OFFICER COLLINS: Then, get ready to die now. !

GROUP LEADER: No, please, give me few minutes to commune with Him and right my wrongs. Please, I beg of you.

OFFICER COLLINS: I am sorry I do not have that luxury. You either live now or die now.

(The gunmen cork their guns and aim it at the Group Leader. He kneels with a bowed head and begins to pray)

GROUP LEADER: I am sorry for all my sins, Lord Jesus! I have been a disgraceful child, an unrepentant sinner, yet singing your praises all the time, covering my dirty inner with a loud camouflaged services on Your Altar. Forgive my atrocities, Jesus. Have mercy, Jesus. When I die, let me see Your face.
(Then, he begins to sing with his hands raised up reverently)
What can wash away my sin?
Nothing but the blood of Jesus;
What can make me whole again? Nothing but the blood of Jesus.

Oh! precious is the flow
That makes me white as snow; No other fount I know,
Nothing but the blood of Jesus.

(There is relative brief silence, as the Group Leader kneels with his head, praying. Officer Collins turns round and gives signals to his gunmen. They all turn and walking towards the exit. Group Leader opens his eyes and see them walking away.)

GROUP LEADER: Eh! Officer! Officer!
(Officer Collins pauses and turns back to look at him)

OFFICER COLLINS: I refuse to kill again. You are free. Run to wherever you can find safety.

GROUP LEADER: No, Officer..! No! My mind is made up to go home tonight..., please, don't do this to me...I want to see my Lord, this night...The Only place of safety is in the presence of my Lord. Please...Command your men.

OFFICER COLLINS: No, Brother. I shall give no further command to kill. I have killed enough and seen the difference between dying for Him and living for self. I am beginning to envy you. Where are all of you eager to go, that many of you are not afraid to die? I have seen people dying with smiles on their faces. I have seen people singing and dancing with eagerness to go and meet their Lord. Only some few foolish ones fear losing their lives. And see you here, begging us to send you to go and meet your Master…Is it not amazing? Can I meet your Master? Can I be forgiven? Can I obtain mercy? Is it possible for Him to save a wretched and terrible soul like mine?

GROUP LEADER: (*still on his kneels*) Ah! Officer, He came to the world purposely to shed His blood and die as a huge sacrifice for the redemption of the whole world. He has already paid the price for the Salvation of the whole world. The Word of God says in John 3:16 "For God so loved the world that He gave His only begotten Son, that whoever believes in Him should not perish but have everlasting life.

OFFICER COLLINS: Has all my Godless acts not given me over to condemnation already? A wretched and wasted life that I lived.

GROUP LEADER: No, Officer. The Word of God further says in Verse 17-18 *For God did not send His Son into the world to condemn the world, but that the world through Him might be saved. He who believes in Him is not condemned; but he who does not believe is condemned already, because he has not believed in the name of the only begotten Son of God.* If you would confess your sins and accept Him as your Lord and Saviour, you will be free of all Condemnations and your name would be written in the Book of Life.

OFFICER COLLINS: (*emotionally*) I am done! I am done with observing one Godless regulation of labeling the Jesus People, the national security risk and obeying the instructions to take them down wherever they are found unless they switch camps and turn their backs to the Jesus, they believe him. I am done! I am done killing joyful people who are eager to see their Master, while my heart is full of concoction of evils. How soon can this be? How do I get connected to Him? How shall I get saved?

GROUP LEADER: The Word of God says in Romans 10:8-11 *"The word is near you, in your mouth and in your heart": that if you confess with your mouth the Lord Jesus and believe in your heart that God has raised Him from the dead, you will be*

saved. For with the heart one believes unto righteousness, and with the mouth confession is made unto salvation. For the Scripture says, "Whoever believes on Him will not be put to shame"

OFFICER COLLINS: Is that all? That looks so cheap and simply to be true.

GROUP LEADER: The Way of Salvation looks simply but the price is huge and heavy. The Son of God died on the Cross to purchase the Eternal Salvation for as many as would accept Him as Lord and Saviour and commit their lives into His hand.

OFFICER COLLINS: (*turns to his gunmen*) Is any of you guys also willing to accept Jesus as his Lord and Saviour? (*Silence as the men stand hesitantly. Then, two of them step forward and signify*)

OFFICER COLLINS: As you can see, I am happy I am not alone in this wise decision.

GROUP LEADER: Can you all knee down with me as I lead you to the arms of the Lord Jesus Christ?

(The Officer and the two gunmen kneel in front of the kneeling Group Leader as they all join their hands together. The remaining two gunmen turn round and walks out of the room.)

GROUP LEADER: Can you say these prayers after me: My Lord Jesus Christ,

ALL: My Lord Jesus Christ.

GROUP LEADER: I come to You today, please, forgive me all my Sins, and wash me clean with your precious Blood. .... I accept
You as my Lord and Saviour today. ....Please, write my Name
in the Book of Life. ....And come into my Heart and take over
my life...

(The other two gunmen that left came inside again followed by the Area Commander and his two guards. He sees Officer Collins and two gunmen on their knees in front of the Group Leader.)

AREA COMMANDER: (*alarmed*) What! Officer Collins, can you explain to me what is going on here? Why are you and these officers on your knees?

OFFICER COLLINS: We just gave our lives to Jesus, Sir. We got converted.

AREA COMMANDER: (*still in shock*) Come again, please. You just did what?

OFFICER COLLINS: Our sins just got forgiven and we have confessed Jesus Christ as our Lord and Saviour.

AREA COMMANDER: But you know the rules, Officer Collins.

OFFICER COLLINS: Yes, Commander. You accept Jesus, you die. You deny Him, you live. (The kneeling gunmen are already in tears and sobbing)

AREA COMMANDER: And you guy, you sure know what you are doing? Because I will take your confessional statement now. (*He turns to Group Leader*) And you, shall we start with you? Who is Jesus to you? You Accept Him you die; you deny Him you live.

GROUP LEADER: You are wrong, Commander. You accept Jesus, you live forever and ever in Heaven. You deny Him, you die forever and ever in everlasting fire of Hell. So, I put the question to you, do you accept Jesus Christ as your Lord and Saviour or not? In John 3:36, the Word of God says: He who believes in the Son has everlasting life; and he who does not believe the Son shall not see life, but the wrath of God abides on him." So, you see, if you want to live and have everlasting life, Believe, and accept the Lord Jesus Christ as the Son of God. But if not, the wrath of God abided on you.

AREA COMMANDER: (*angrily*) Stop throwing the questions back at me! Are you for Jesus or against Him?

GROUP LEADER: (*begins to sing with a broad smile*)

*Blessed assurance, Jesus is mine! Oh, what a foretaste of glory
divine! Heir of salvation, purchase of God,
Born of His Spirit, washed in His blood*

Chorus:
This is my story, this is my song Praising my Saviour all day long.

*(He points his pistol to him at close range, and fires. Group Leader
sinks on the floor, as he holds his chest oozing blood. He continues
mumbling the hymn as he falls lower and lower on the floor)*

GROUP LEADER: (continues) *This is my story, this is my song,
Praising my Saviour all day long.*

*(He finishes the hymn and stays motionless. Officer Collins looks at
his motionless body and begins to shout aloud)*

OFFICER COLLINS: Jesus...! Jesus...! Jesus...! Good evening, Jesus!
Thank you, Jesus! They are about to kill me. ....
Jesus!

(Gunman I who is in silent tears begins to sing with lower voice)

GUNMAN I: *(Sings)*
Jesus loves me, yes, I know, the Bible tells me so,

I will love Him for ever, For the Bible tells me so.

(The Gunman II kneeling beside him picks up the chorus with him)

GUNMAN II: (sings with Gunman I)
Yes, Jesus Loves me.

Yes, Jesus loves me. Yes, Jesus loves me, For the Bible tells me so.

AREA COMMANDER: (*To his Gunmen*) You know what to do. Do your job.

(He turns round and begins to walk out as the Gunmen begin to spray them with a rain of bullets.)

***

IF YOU DENY HIM, YOU LIVE.
IF YOU CONFESS HIM, YOU DIE. WHAT WOULD YOU DO?

Matthew 10:32-33
Therefore, whoever confesses Me before men, him I will also confess before My Father who is in heaven. But whoever denies Me before men, him I will also deny before My Father who is in heaven.

Epilogue

It is not until a gun is put to your head. It is not until you stand at the execution stakes It is not until some soldiers of the Anti-God approach you with riffles.

On daily bases, numerous Children of the Kingdom are betraying the King that died for them to live.

They denied Him in their Offices and Places of works. They feel ashamed to be called the Children of the King. They feel inferior to be branded with the Master. They feel uncomfortable raising the Flag of their Salvation! They denied Him when they are called upon to stand for Him.

They are in the Police Force! Betrayers and Traitors of the Master! They are in the Civil Service! Rebels who turn against the lifestyles of the Kingdom for a morsel of bread.

Defectors!
Deserters!

They join forces with the Children of Darkness to do Pen Robberies! They turn their back against the Lord amidst their friends and live their lives immorally!

He had planted all His children on all realms of the nations. To shine the light! To hold the Candle Lights in the midst of the Gross Darkness! God had made the Provisions available for enough Light all around! But many Lights are kept under the Bushels. Many lamps are quenched that they may mot shine in the dark!

When you join hands to commit evil, you betray the Master!
When you turn around to live in deliberate sins, you defect to the other side!
When you turn around to stand against the course of the Kingdom, you become a rebel!

When you decide to stop running your race of the Kingdom and begin to live according to the dictates of your sinful desires, you become a Traitor!

There are many Believers who are passing through the Persecutions. And dying for their faith!

But there are many others who are Compromising Faiths and Stands without the Guns!

They are Traitors too! They are Betrayals too! They are Deserters too!
They are Standing down in the Darkest Night!

Section Two

A POETRY'S EMBRACE OF MIKE BAMILOYE'S DARKEST NIGHT

Olumide Oki

In the realm where poetry intertwines with the realm of the theatrical, I invite you to embark on a profound journey through the pages of this section. This poetic anthology holds a captivating embrace, inspired by the essence of Mike Bamiloye's renowned play, "Darkest Night." With an eloquent fusion of words, it delves into the depths of emotions, shadows, and revelations that unfold under the cloak of a desolate night.

Within these verses, you will find yourself immersed in the solemnity and solitude of a night's descent. The title itself conjures images of darkness stretching its fingers across the world, casting a melancholic veil upon all that it touches. It is in this very darkness that the power of poetry emerges, capturing the essence of Bamiloye's play and infusing it with lyrical resonance.

As you venture further into the realm of this section, you will bear witness to the evocative embrace between poetry and the dramatic narrative. Each line, crafted with meticulous artistry, unravels the intricate layers of emotions experienced within the depths of the darkest night.

It is a journey of exploration, where the Spirit becomes a guiding light, illuminating the shadows and shedding insight into the human condition.

Within these pages, you will discover the intertwining threads of despair, hope, redemption, and introspection. The poems pay homage to Bamiloye's masterpiece, capturing the essence of his characters, their struggles, and their ultimate search for meaning and salvation. Through vivid descriptions, vivid imagery, and evocative metaphors, the verses encapsulate the very essence of the play, breathing new life into its themes and messages.

This sectioninvites you to immerse yourself in the tapestry of emotions, to contemplate the depths of the night, and to embrace the poetic interpretation of Mike Bamiloye's "Darkest Night" play. It is a testament to the power of words, the resonance of art, and the enduring connection between poetry and the dramatic narrative. Prepare to embark on a journey that transcends time and space, where the night's descent becomes a canvas for poetic expression and literary enchantment.

Olumide Oki June 6, 2023

One

INVADED BY CHAOS

In the small town of Agbamu, a
night of despair, Chaos and
pandemonium filled the air.
Gunshots rang out, screams
echoed around, A scene of
terror, sorrow, and tears
profound.

Religious extremists had invaded
the place, Leaving the community in
a state of disgrace. Men, women,
children, and elders in fear,
Scattered like leaves, running,
shedding a tear.

Amid the cacophony of gunshots and
cries, People dashed in panic, their
hopes compromised. The darkness of
night only heightened the fright, As the
wounded groaned and the dying lost
their fight.

Into an uncompleted building, a man
named Kenny, Guided his family, through

the chaos and frenzy.
His wife, Tobi, her hands trembling in
distress, Shielding their youngest, trying
to calm their distress.

Kenny's arms held their two children
so tight, His heart pounding, his brow
drenched in sweat and fright. Each step they
took, their tears mingled with dread, As they
sought refuge from the nightmarish spread.

The moon watched in silence,
casting a pale light, Illuminating
scenes of desperation, a woeful
sight. The uncompleted building
stood like a fortress, A temporary
haven in this night's cruel duress.

Within its walls, shadows danced and
swayed, Whispering tales of anguish,
as if memories replayed. The sounds of
gunshots seeped through the cracks, A
constant reminder of the world's brutal
attacks.

Kenny and Tobi, their hearts heavy with
dread, Held their children close, shielding
them from the dread. They whispered
words of comfort, a soothing balm, As the
chaos outside continued its alarming
psalm.

The youngest child, eyes wide with
fear, Looked to his parents, seeking
solace near. Tobi kissed his forehead,
her touch gentle and warm, Promising
safety, shielding him from harm.

Still in the heart of the community, chaos
roams, Pandemonium reigns, disarray it foams.
Sporadic gunshots continues to pierce the
night's calm air, Screams and wailing blend, a
symphony of despair.

A night of sorrow, tears
cascade like rain, The world
seems broken, riddled with
pain.
Gunshots persist, tearing the deadened
night, Amidst the clamor, groans of the
wounded's plight.

A darkest night descends, a
wailing night, A trial of faith,
where hopes take flight.
The mighty falter, their strength
laid bare, While the weaklings
rise, their courage rare.

Two

IN THE MIDST OF TENSION

In the midst of tension, heavy in
the air, Kenny whispered to his
wife, a fervent prayer. Fear and
determination intermingled
within, As they faced danger,
their faith would begin.

Tears streamed down Tobi's face,
etching pain, Echoing the loss, the
heartache's refrain.
Yet, amidst the sorrow, a chilling truth
arose, Footsteps approached, their
hiding place exposed.

Esther sought solace in her father's
embrace, Whispering through tears,
fear etched on her face. They had
been found, pursuers closing in,
Their lives hanging by a perilous thin.

With urgency, Kenny shushed his
daughter's plea, Silence their ally in
their bid to be free.
Behind a barricade, they crawled in

despair, Seeking refuge from
danger's lurking snare.

Suddenly, armed men stormed
into the room, Guns held
ominously, shrouded in gloom.
They pushed a wounded man,
battered and weak, Bloodied and
bruised, his body bespeak.

The family remained hidden, still
as stone, Dependent on stealth,
on the unknown. Eavesdropping
on the exchanges ahead, Their
very existence suspended by a
thread.

A corporal sneered, contempt
tainting his tone, Addressing the
wounded, in a voice cold as stone.
Impatience seeped from another's
gaze,
His gun dangerously close, fear's wicked maze.

"Joel," he spat the name, the gun
held near, "Enough with the games,
no room for fear. Who is Jesus
Christ to you? Renounce your faith,
Time is fleeting, decide on your
life's wraith."

Trembling and weeping, Joel
struggled to speak, His words a

desperate plea, his voice weak.
Fear clouded his mind, the right
words a haze, The corporal
relentless, demanding his ways.

Joel stammered and faltered,
nearing the end, Attempting to
utter what he couldn't defend.
But as terror gripped him, his
voice grew loud,
Pleading, begging the corporal, his heart unbowed.

Behind the barricade, the
family remained, Held their
breath, their lives constrained.
The suffocating silence, a weight on their souls,
As the countdown neared, they clung to their roles.

But in the depths of his darkest
hour's toll, Joel clung to hope,
to a heavenly console. He called
upon Jesus, his voice raised in
plea,
Beseeching salvation, from darkness set free.

Desperation fueled each word
that he spoke, His faith waging
war, against darkness's cloak. In
the hidden confines, their hearts
tightly knit, They waited, hoping,
for a divine permit.

In the face of peril, their resolve

held strong, United in faith,
defying what was wrong.
For in the depths of despair, a
light may arise, Guiding their
steps, unveiling truth from lies.

Will their prayers be answered, their
souls set free, Or will darkness prevail,
engulfing their plea?
Only time will tell, as their fate unfolds,
In this moment of anguish, where hope beholds.

Three

The Blade Of The Corporal

The corporal's voice, devoid of
compassion's grace, Cut through the
air, a blade in the dark place.
Joel's pleas grew desperate, a
mixture of despair, Seeking
salvation, his Savior's name in
prayer.

As the countdown neared its final decree,
Joel's trembling voice rang out,
resolute and free. Professing his
belief, his faith held strong,
Defying the corporal, admitting where he belonged.

The second corporal, impatient
and cruel, Moved forward, his
intentions a vile fuel. Mocking
Joel's faith, sneering with disdain,
The room's tension peaked, a
moment of pain.

In an act of courage, Joel found his
voice, Strengthened by his belief,
making a choice.

He declared Jesus not bound by
hell's embrace, But residing in
heaven, awaiting his grace.

The power in his words, a testament
of zeal, Resonated through the
room, a devotion so real. Taken
aback by Joel's fervor and fire,
The corporal succumbed to frustration's desire.

He raised his gun, a cruel smile
on his face, Pulled the trigger,
ending Joel's earthly race. The
sound of the gunshot shattered
the air, Joel fell, life
extinguished, his spirit laid bare.

The corporal, in callous contempt, did
not cease, Spitting on Joel's body, a
display of his vile release. Hidden
behind the barricade, Kenny and his
kin, Trembled as they listened to the
departing sin.

The weight of the scene, a
harrowing sight, Left them
shaken, filled with despair's
might. Kenny's wife, anguish in
her voice, expressed, Fears and
uncertainty, their future
oppressed.

Kenny, frayed nerves and heart
worn thin, Sought to provide
strength, to reassure within.
Gathering his children, holding
them near,
He urged them to remain steadfast, without fear.

Tears trickled on his cheek, filled with woe,
He urged them, find solace, let
God's love flow. Though shadows
may haunt their every stride, With
Jesus as guide, they'd conquer
and ride.

Esther, trembling with fear,
uncertainty's veil, Questioned the
looming threat, death's dark trail.
Kenny, voice trembling yet
determined to fight, Encouraged her
strength, to be her siblings' light.

Their faith unyielding, no matter
the cost, They'd stand with Jesus,
no matter the exhaust. Fear and
uncertainty swirled in their space,
But their allegiance to the Lord would leave no trace.

As despair filled their hidden place,
Kenny's wife, Peer through a small
opening, encountered strife.
Recoiling in shock, terror etched in
her cry, Desperation's plea, piercing

through the sky.

Kenny turned, alarmed by her
reaction's bloom, To witness the
Sentry officer's entrance in gloom.
Accompanied by soldiers from their
prior plight, Tension heightened,
fears unleashed in the night.

Silence fell heavy, their breath held
in suspense, The air crackled,
charged with uncertain events.
The room's walls whispered of their
destiny's plight, As the Sentry officer
approached, cloaked in fright.

Four
TREMBLING HEARTS

In a distant dwelling, the Andersons dwell,
A family in anguish, trapped in a
fearful spell. Mr. and Mrs.
Anderson, their kids by their side,
Huddled in fright, uncertain where
to hide.

They gather by the dining set, hearts racing fast,
As the night outside echoes with
screams and blasts. Gunshots sporadic,
shouts of dismay,
Creating an atmosphere fraught with dismay.

Mr. Anderson rushes upstage with
great haste, Joining his family, the
fear on his face.
He whispers to his wife, his voice
quivering low, Someone has
entered, their peace now in tow.

A figure he recognizes, Simon, the
Choir Leader, But with him, three
others, their intentions unclear.
Worried and nervous, Mr. Anderson

imparts,
To his wife and children, the need to depart.

But Mrs. Anderson, filled with
courage and might, Refuses to flee,
standing by her husband's side.
She urges the children, Temmy and Laolu,
To retreat to their room, a hiding spot they pursue.

In a corner they huddle, seeking
safety's embrace, As a loud bang on
the door sends shivers in place. Knocks
follow, relentless, demanding entry,
Mr. Anderson approaches, his steps somewhat wary.

Unlocking the door, he peeks out in dread,
To find Simon outside, his face filled
with dread. Apologies stumble from
Simon's trembling lips, And soldiers
enter, their presence eclipsed.

Confirming Mr. Anderson's identity, they explain,
Their mission to search for religious leaders,
to cause pain. Pastors, reverends, and the
faithful they seek,
Their families too, to subject them to bleak.

Simon, under duress, confesses
his betrayal, Under threat of his
life, he revealed their trail. He led
the soldiers to the Andersons'
home, His own survival, the

reason they now roam.

The soldiers proclaim their grim
ultimatum, Denounce their faith or
face a brutal termination. Simon,
commended for making the "right"
choice, Providing the information
with a trembling voice.

Now comes a question, with
consequences grave, Demanding Mr.
Anderson to speak and be brave.
They ask who Jesus Christ is to his
soul,
The tension mounts, taking its terrible toll.

Before he can answer, Simon
interrupts with haste, Warning against
words that would be a waste.
For confessing Jesus, the Son of
God divine, Means death in an
instant, no chance to decline.

Mr. Anderson is stunned, his mind in a
whirl, Contemplating the fate of this
unforgiving world. But his wife, Martha,
her faith resolute and strong,
Steps forward boldly, declaring she'll never be wrong.

Her steadfast faith in Jesus
she proclaims, Unyielding to
renounce, she maintains.

The soldiers grow restless, their
weapons raised, Seeking a reply,
their voices phased.

Five

THE BATTLE OF FAITH

Amidst the tension, a struggling sound
breaks through, A young man, bloodied,
appears, his face askew.
Segun, in desperation, stumbles and falls,
At Mr. Anderson's feet, his voice filled with calls.

He reveals their hiding place, the
church vestry, Their discovery
resulting in tragedy.
Anthony and Kemi lost to the cruel hand,
And Segun, tortured but strong, managed to withstand.

Shock and anguish fill Mr. Anderson's eyes,
As one soldier admonishes Segun,
no disguise. The sentry officer
arrives, stern and grim,
With another officer, their chances looking dim.

They bring Segun under control, his fate in
their hands, Urging him to renounce his
faith's holy demands.
Escape seems impossible, a fleeting dream,
As the sentry officer warns, time grows gleam.

But faith is a fire that refuses to wane,
And Segun, battered yet resolute,
won't entertain The idea of forsaking
what he holds dear,
His convictions unwavering, crystal clear.

In a world of darkness
and despair, Where
persecution fills the
air,
Segun still stood tall,
unyielding and brave, Facing
the sentry officer, his life to
save.

The officer's voice stern and harsh,
Demanded a confession, a renouncing of the
Lord's touch, But Segun, steadfast, held his
ground,
With faith in his heart, his voice resound.

"I have been crucified with
Christ," he said, His words filled
with strength, his soul unwed,
For Christ lived within him, a
guiding light,
In his flesh, he lived by faith, not by sight.

The officer's anger flared, his patience frayed,
He menaced Segun with death, a
price to be paid. Yet Segun beamed,

a serenity unfurled,
For he glimpsed his true abode, where his soul would
be hurled.

"I see... Angels...
everywhere," he spoke, A
vision of hope, beyond life's
yoke,
But the officer, blind to the truth
revealed, Dismissed it as a
hallucination, unconcealed.

Undeterred, Segun continued his plea,
"I see... Angels... everywhere,"
his spirit free, But the officer,
consumed by his rage, Silenced
Segun with a bullet, ending his
stage.

Mr. Anderson's heart pounded
in his chest, As Segun's life
ended, his soul put to rest.
Grief and terror collided, consuming his being,
His thoughts a tumultuous storm, endlessly careening.

Visions of Segun's lifeless form haunted his mind,
His trembling hands, evidence of fear he
couldn't bind. He questioned his choices,
his role in this plight,
The weight of responsibility, a burden so tight.

A Home Shattered

Still in the Andersons' home, sorrow
filled the air, As Temmy and Laolu, in
hiding, were aware, Their parents'
lives taken, a cruel blow,
Their tears flowing, their fear starting to grow.

They trembled with grief, their young hearts torn,
As they witnessed the tragedy, their
innocence shorn, For the gunshot
echoed, its reverberation wide, Leaving
them shaken, nowhere to hide.

The sentry officer, cold and
detached, Continued his duty,
his soul unmatched,
Demanding confessions,
ignoring the pain, The
Andersons knelt, their faith in
vain.

But Martha, defiant,
refused to comply, Her
voice resolute, reaching
the sky,

"For me and my house, we shall
serve the Lord," She proclaimed,
her conviction untoward.

Her husband, Pastor Anderson,
pleaded in fear, Begging her to
relent, to make things clear, But
Martha stood firm, her faith
unwavering,
Ready to face death, her soul undeterred, unerring.

The officer, infuriated, shouted
his demand, To renounce
Jesus, to let go of His hand,
But Martha, with tears streaming
down her face, Accepted death as a
friend, her final embrace.

"I will wait for you on the other
side," she cried, Her words filled
with hope, her spirit amplified,
To whom it may concern, she
proclaimed her belief, Not to deny her
faith, for in eternity they'd meet.

The officer, consumed by his
anger and pride, Raised his gun,
ending Martha's stride,
Her life extinguished, her voice silenced,
Yet her spirit soared, her faith undiminished.

In anguish, Laolu and Temmy

emerged, From their hiding
place, their hearts surged,
Their parents slain before their
young eyes, Their cries of grief,
piercing the skies.

Their father, grief-stricken, questioned
their choice, Why did they come out,
why raise their voice,
But the children, brave, shared their
genuine voice, Of Jesus, their Savior,
their eternal rejoice.

The officer, surprised by their
unwavering stance, Mocked their
defiance, denying their chance,
He aimed his gun at the innocent souls,
And shot them down, their spirits ascending in roles.

Mr. Anderson crumbled, his spirit crushed,
His heartache insurmountable, his
pain brushed Against the jagged
edges of his shattered soul, As
grief engulfed him, taking its toll.

He knelt by the lifeless bodies of his
children dear, Their innocent faces
etched with sorrow, with fear. Their
laughter silenced, their dreams untold,
He wept for their loss, his heart painfully cold.

His voice, once vibrant, now hollow

and weak, Uttered lamentations,
words he couldn't speak. The
weight of despair, an anchor on his
chest,
As he clung to memories, the ones he loved best.

Seven
A Faith Betrayed

In a corner, Simon crouches,
consumed by fear, Bursting into
tears, his anguish sincere.
"Oh, God!" he cries, his voice filled
with despair, Seeking solace in a
world so unfair.

But the sentry officer,
stern and cold, Lashes
out, his words
uncontrolled,
"Shut your damn mouth!" he angrily
commands, Simon trembles,
gripping tightly to his strands.

With fear in his eyes, he utters
his confession, "Yes, sir...yes,
sir...I did, without question."
Acknowledging his guilt, his
voice quivering, In this moment,
his faith is withering.

A soldier confirms his self-accusation,
"He has made his own confession," a

declaration. Yet the sentry officer
demands once more, "Renounce
your faith, let it be known for sure."

Trembling, Simon stammers, his heart
pounding, "Yes, sir... Jesus Christ, I
renounce You," resounding. The sentry
officer interrupts, unrelenting,
"How long have you followed this faith, dissenting?"

Simon's voice shakes as he
answers, sincere, "This year
marks the fourteenth, sir, I
fear." But the officer's wrath
knows no bounds,
After fourteen years, Simon's faith he grounds.

"You can't be trusted, you're not
worthy," he shouts, His judgment
casting shadows, casting doubts.
Simon pleads, his voice shaking
with despair, "No! I mean it... I
mean every word I share."

He explains his reasons, his voice filled with
pain, Disappointment and unanswered
prayers, a heavy chain. "I've waited for
crucial things, in vain," he cries,
A faith tested, a spirit left to agonize.

The officer scorns him, his judgment
unleashed, "If I were your Jesus, I

would deny you, beast!" Simon cries
out, a cry of anguish profound,
But the officer's heart remains stone cold, astound.

And in a moment of chaos, a
moment of strife, Simon lunges
forward, fighting for his life.
He grabs Soldier 1, holding
him in his grip, Defying his
fate, refusing to submit.

Soldier 1 commands Soldier 2 to
stand down, A temporary
reprieve, a moment of resound.
But the sentry officer, shocked
and appalled, Halts the
impending tragedy, words
recalled.

With tears streaming down his face,
Simon pleads, "Please, you can't do
this, I've followed your leads!" But the
officer's heart remains unmoved,
As the squad prepares, their actions proved.

In a flash, Soldier 2's gun points
with precision, Simon falls to the
ground, a tragic decision.
The officer commends their
ruthless display, "Good one,
officers," he coldly does say.

As Simon lies lifeless, a civilian, no more,
The sentry officer looks upon him,
blood and gore. His attention shifts, a
new target in sight,
Mr. Anderson, marked for an execution's plight.

Eight

A Chamber of Pain

In a chamber of pain, where
shadows dance, A young man's
agony, a gruesome trance.
Four military men, with hearts
of stone, Inflict torment upon
him, flesh and bone.

His undershirt, soaked in
crimson red, As he lies on
the floor, his spirit bled.
Pinned down by two, his
struggle in vain, While the
others revel in his cries of
pain.

A pair of pliers, sharp and gleaming,
In the tormentor's hand, a
nightmare teaming. He clamps
them down, a vicious assault,
As the young man's screams fill the somber vault.

A wretched groan, a plea for
release, But his cries fall on
ears devoid of peace. With

sadistic pleasure, 2IC Collins
stands,
The Regimental Sergeant Major, his demands.

"We removed one nail, a fraction of
your hand, And we'll continue until
you cannot withstand. Until your
eyes are dry, no tears remain,
We'll torment your spirit, break you, and maim."

The tortured man, his voice
strained with pain, Begs for
mercy, but it's all in vain.
Collins produces a document, a
sinister plea, For affirmation, to
fuel their wicked spree.

Marvelous Hezokwat, his name in ink,
From East Africa, his origin they know and
not just think. Choir master, his talent
renowned,
But his faith, they seek to confound.

"We need celebrities to deny
their creed, To make our
work easier, plant the seed.
Thus one nail won't suffice, we'll pierce
through tough, Unveiling your faith as a
mere bluff."

Face to face, Collins leans in near,
His eyes filled with venom,

hatred clear. "Who is Jesus
Christ to you?" he spits, His
voice dripping with malice,
bit by bit.

Through the pain, the tortured
man holds fast, His defiance, his
faith, unsurpassed.
He speaks of the Son, the
Most High God, Each word
resounding, his spirit shod.

But Collins, consumed by
rage's flame, Unleashes a
whip, to scar and maim.
Lashes rain down, his back a canvas raw,
Yet his spirit remains unbroken, standing tall.

With every strike, his beliefs are
proclaimed, Jesus Christ, the
Lord, forever named.
The room trembles with his resolute plea,
As faith pierces through darkness, wild and free.

But Collins, fueled by fury's cruel might,
Ends the torment, darkness blotting
out the light. A cold act, a gun raised,
poised to kill,
The tortured man's fate, a foreboding chill.

With a pull of the trigger, a
gunshot's dread, The young

man falls, a lifeless thread.
Blood spills forth, staining the
unforgiving floor, His spirit
released, his suffering no more.

In the aftermath, silence
heavy and grim, His final
defiant words etched
within.
A life extinguished by
brutality's might, Yet his
faith blazes on, a beacon of
light.

Nine

FEAR IN THE SACRED PLACE

Inside the church's sacred
space, so vast, Fear grips the
worshippers, shadows cast.
Fifteen souls gathered, faces filled
with dread, Tears fall, trembling
bodies, apprehension spread.

The church's door, tightly locked,
stands firm, As Pastor Larry,
dressed saintly, begins to affirm. In
hushed tones, he speaks the Word
divine, Isaiah 43:2, a promise, a
lifeline.

"When you pass through waters, I'll be
with you, Rivers won't overflow, the
flame won't scorch you." Brethren
urged to calm down, trust in the Lord,
For He is a mighty warrior, His shield and sword.

But Brother Alex, panic-
stricken, distraught, His wife
and children lost, his heart taut.
Running towards the church, they

disappeared, Fears surge, his
anguish, his soul seared.

A desperate banging, loud
upon the door, Hope surges
within, anticipation soars.
Brother Alex believes it's his
family outside, Eager to enter,
relief to abide.

Pastor Larry, cautious, holds
him back, "What if it's not
them?" his voice on track.
Alex's hope tempered with
uncertainty, Fearful of the
dangers that may be.

But what if they're in danger, standing
at the brink? Alex's hands tremble, he
cannot rethink.
He rushes to the door, people
hiding in fear, Unlocking,
opening, a moment unclear.

The door pushed in, a lady's frantic race,
She shuts it quickly, seeking
solace and grace. Angie, in
distress, pleads for their aid,
Soldiers approach, their presence
forbade.

Panic spreads, people scurrying to hide,

Mama Rowland speaks with concern,
her voice tied. "Are you leading them
here, endangering our lives?" Accusing
Angie, suspicion in their eyes.

"No!" she cries, seeking Pastor Larry's gaze,
"I never knew of your presence,
this holy place. I banged the door,
seeking refuge and safety,
Unaware of your plight, seeking
sanctuary."

Displeased, Pastor Larry
questions her move, What has
she done, the risks she may
prove. Angie defends her faith,
her plea sincere, Church as a
refuge, love for Christ held dear.

But Mr. David, with sharp
words, condemns, Unwise
decisions, danger that
condemns.
Leading pursuers to the
church's door, Endangering
lives, wisdom she ignored.

Soldiers approach, with
purpose, in control, A dynamite
hung, a deadly toll.
A spark ignites, fear propels all
to hide, Except Pastor Larry,

standing with stride.

Soldiers advance, their strides resound, Entering the church, their presence profound. Tension fills the air, hearts quicken their beat, As the tale unfurls, its grip remains fleet.

Ten

TRAPPED WITHIN THE AUDITORIUM

Within the auditorium, a
tense affair, 2IC Collins and
his officers declare,
Surrounded, trapped, their
voices stern,
Warning the worshippers, causing hearts to churn.

A public address cone
firmly in hand, Collins
steps forward, in
command.
His words, a threat that
hangs in the air, A leap of
escape, perilous and unfair.

Pastor Larry, cautious,
approaches the scene, His voice
shaky, his demeanor keen.
Attempting to reason, to find
common ground, In this perilous
moment, chaos all around.

But Collins, stern and
unyielding, Demands

respect, his power
revealing. He orders the
hiding souls to emerge, No
room for negotiation, no
safe surge.

Pastor Larry, defensive, tries to explain,
In this time of fear and self-
preservation's reign. Each man for
himself, seeking security's hold, He
pleads for dialogue, a story yet
untold.

But Collins, gripping the P.A
system tight, Broadcasts his
ultimatum with all his might. A
countdown, a warning, a final
decree, Death awaits those
who refuse to be free.

The P.A system back to his mouth,
A threat resounds, striking fear from
north to south. No chance to speak, no
plea for mercy,
His men ready to execute with swift accuracy.

Pastor Larry, stuttering, at a
loss for words, Fidgets in
desperation, like captured
birds. Time ticks away, tension
on the rise,
As the countdown continues, no compromise.

Collins, determined, removes
the P.A, Facing the pastor, his
gaze in disarray. Promising to
be the one to take a life,
Should any of his men cause
further strife.

Pastor Larry, on the edge of
despair, Utters a feeble
sound, caught in the snare.
But the countdown resumes, no
time to stall, Fear spreads like
wildfire, gripping one and all.

In a flurry of chaos, Pastor Larry
runs, Shouting, calling for
everyone, his voice stuns. The
hiding souls emerge, screaming in
fear, Their cries and wails, echoes
loud and clear.

The auditorium fills with terrified cries,
As the worshippers face their
darkest skies. The matter
unfolds, tensions intertwine,
In this gripping moment, lives on the line.

Eleven

DYING FOR THE LORD

In a scene of despair and
trembling fear, Pastor Larry's
voice quivers, shedding a tear.
His accent changes, a foreign
lilt,
As he cries out, his spirit nearly wilt.

Surprised, 2IC Collins
questions his tone, Phonetics
transformed, a tale unknown.
Pastor Larry stammers,
nervous and weak, A foreign
education, his voice meek.

Collins demands a name, full
and clear, Mr. David speaks,
respect he holds dear. But
Collins shuts him down with a
rebuke, Silencing his voice,
like a tightening noose.

Pastor Larry steps forward,
to represent, His
congregation, their fate to

lament.
Olanrewaju Akinmoogunje, he
proclaims, His full name,
surprising those in the game.

The decree is established, a
new command, No room for
Jesus, a hostile demand.
Those who stand firm will face
certain death, While the ones who
renounce will draw a breath.

Fear engulfs the crowd, tears
stream down, As Collins' words
echo with a haunting sound. A
collective "yes, sir" escapes their
lips, Quivering, shaking, like
fragile ships.

Collins turns to the pastor, a
critical test, To make a
decision, for all the rest.
Confess or deny, Jesus
as their Lord, A life-or-
death choice, a heavy
chord.

Pastor Larry struggles,
his words fail, Opening
his mouth, a silent wail.
Collins grows impatient, time
ticks away, The congregation

prays, hoping for a sway.

But Angie steps forward, her
voice breaking, Seeking to
intervene, her heart awaking.
Collins grants her
permission to speak, A
glimmer of hope, her plea
to seek.

With faith in her voice, she
addresses the crowd, Sharing the
promise of mansions, unbowed.
Heaven's abode, a place
for them all, If death
awaits, they'll answer the
call.

Oyadare interrupts, with
doubts in his voice, Dismissing
the promise, making a choice.
He renounces Jesus, with bold
disdain, Believing the promise to
be nothing but a feign.

Collins chuckles,
amusement in his eyes,
Oyadare steps aside, his
decision flies.
Dividing the crowd, those
who believe, And those who
don't, their souls deceived.

People shift slowly, choosing
their side, The Lady's side,
where faith will abide. Fifteen
souls stand firm, prepared to
die, While six embrace doubt,
their faith awry.

Pastor Larry remains at the
center, still, A decision
unclear, a heart to distill.
Collins grows furious, raising
his gun, Demanding a choice,
before the rising sun.

With a calm resolve, Pastor
Larry moves, To the side of
doubt, his faith he proves.
Shocked whispers fill the
trembling air, As Angie
questions his denial, a
despair.

The pastor's explanation falls on
their ears, Wisdom guides his
choice, allaying their fears. From
the Elders Book of Wisdom, he
claims, An escape from the fight,
wisdom proclaims.

But Angie's
astonishment lingers

still, Seeking the truth,
her spirit to fill.
Is wisdom found in the
book divine, Or a path
away from God's
design?

Mama Rowland, surprised, speaks
her concern, Dying for the Lord, a
lesson to learn.
But Pastor Larry counters, with
words profound, Wisdom guides, a
purpose profound.

2IC Collins ends the scene, his
decision sealed, Their fate
determined, their hearts
congealed. Angie, in anguish,
speaks her lament,
Pastor Larry denied Jesus, her soul rent.

Twelve

A PROCESSION OF SORROW

In a chilling moment, 2IC takes control,
A whistle blows, the door opens, a
haunting stroll. Two men in red
overalls enter the scene,
Carrying boxes, with an eerie gleam.

The CFI, Classified Freedom
Identification, A symbol of
safety, a mark of salvation.
An instrument, like an
infrared device, Applied
to foreheads, a mark
precise.

The people tremble, tears
streaming down, As the red
patch forms, their faces a
frown. The boxes are closed,
carried away, Leaving behind a
sense of dismay.

With CFI in place, they're
deemed secure, Free to
move, no threats to endure.

But 2IC's command echoes with dread,
All standing for Jesus, into the bus, they're led.

A soldier leads, guiding their way,
Apprehension fills the air, a
disheartening display. They line up,
tears staining their cheeks,
A procession of sorrow, their spirit weak.

Officers and gunmen, they join the ride,
A bus filled with fear, as they
journey wide. Off they go,
towards the execution center,
A destination unknown, a fate
to enter.

Inside the church, anxiety
remains, Pastor and others,
their nerves in chains.
Apprehensive whispers, hearts
beating fast, In this moment of
darkness, their faith is cast.

In a burst of chaos, thugs invade the
sacred space, Their leader, Marley,
unmasks, revealing his face. Pastor
Larry, back to phonetics, tries to
reason, But Marley's anger erupts, a
bitter season.

"Before you see monkey," Marley
screams aloud, His gang responds,

their voices proud.
Disappointed in the pastor,
Marley accuses, Betraying
Jesus, the truth he deduces.

"You! You go say you no
sabi me?" Marley
confronts, his fury plain
to see. Pastor Larry, still
in his linguistic guise, Fails
to recognize Marley's
eyes.

"Speak normal English," the church
members insist, Frustration and
disappointment, they cannot resist.
Marley, disgusted, feels provoked and
vexed, Summoning thugs, he hopes to
protect.

"Gather the local thugs, from
far and wide, To stop the
haggard military's stride.
If we die today, let us die together,
But first, my church, where I used to gather."

"My pastor has denied Jesus,"
Marley exclaims, His gang echoes
the pain, their cries inflame.
But Pastor Larry, sobbing,
attempts to explain, "He who runs
from fight lives to fight again."

Marley scoffs, "Who is your
brother, who cares? My pastor is
fake," he declares in despair.
Singing his name, Marley
ley fills the air, His gang
responds, a chant of
despair.

"If I fight today, it will be in vain,"
he sings, Gang members joining,
the bitter truth it brings. In anger,
Marley points his gun, no time to
talk,
Shoots the pastor, like Judas, with a shocking shock.

The congregation gasps, cries of
anguish rise, Marley, to his gang,
commands their demise. "Let's
tell the alaga to put everyone to
sleep,
This man has weakened me," he says with a deep creep.

As the gang members exit, scattering
in the night, The church trembles in
fear, losing its light.
A tragic scene, with lives shattered
and scattered, A moment of
darkness, a soul deeply tattered.

Thirteen

THE MELODY OF FAITH

In a place adorned with symbols
of dread, Skulls and weapons, a
sight to fill with dread. The
ground, a canvas for blood-
stained bodies, A scene of horror
where darkness embodies.

Soldiers carry the dead, with heavy hearts,
While the Kenny Family, bound to
stakes, imparts, Fear and anguish grip
their every breath,
As officers, guns ready, await their impending death.

Amidst this terror, the others are
brought in, Forced to sit on the floor,
fear etched deep within. Tears mingle
with forced smiles on their faces,
A dance of emotions in these harrowing spaces.

But the Kenny Family, tied and
facing demise, Begin to sing, their
voices reaching the skies. "To
Thee, O Comforter divine," they
start, Praising God's grace with an

unwavering heart.

Their melody carries
through the air, A hymn
of faith, a testament
rare.
"For all Thy grace and pow'r
benign," they sing, In the face of
darkness, their spirits take wing.

"To Thee, whose faithful love had place,
In God's great covenant of grace,"
they embrace. Their voices echo,
defiance in each note,
With Alleluia's chorus, they refuse to be remote.

2IC Collins, in his
commanding tone, Orders
the squad guards to form a
zone. Positions held, guns
ready for the decree, The
tension rises, a moment of
destiny.

"Reload on standby!" 2IC Collins
commands, The anticipation
heavy, the air expands.
And with a final call, the
officers prepare, To unleash
their fire, a deadly affair.

As the hymn reaches its final refrain,

The officers open fire, causing
unimaginable pain. Bullets rain
down, a torrent of despair,
The Christians fall, their lives left threadbare.

The execution complete, the
officers depart, Leaving behind
a scene, a broken heart.
But after a while, a heavenly descent begins,
Angels descend, crowning the martyrs, free from sins.

One by one, they are
adorned with grace, Their
souls lifted, their pain
erased.
In a solemn procession,
they walk along, Guided by
angels, their spirits strong.

Though their earthly journey has
come to an end, Their legacy lives
on, as a message they send.
Their faith and courage, an
eternal flame, Inspiring
generations, in His holy
name.

Fourteen

THE LIVING ROOM'S STANDOFF

In a living room, adorned
with prestige, Decorated
beautifully, a sight to feast.
A man stands,
apprehension in his eyes,
By the electronic cabinet, where secrets lie.

Armed men positioned,
strategic and firm, Their guns
ready, their presence affirm.
As the gunmen walk in, a tense
gaze exchanged, A standoff of
power, both sides unchanged.

A sentry officer, with a faint smile on
his face, Introduces himself, Captain
Effiong with grace. "The Sentinel of
this Area Command," he declares,
"The Eagle Eye, should you require
my cares."

But the reverend, defensive in his
tone, Asserts his faith, not willing
to be overthrown.

"God has given me boldness, a sound
mind," he replies, Intimidation won't work,
he won't compromise.

Captain Effiong questions the
reverend's choice, To arm his men,
to raise his voice.
"Doesn't Jesus defend you?" he queries
with surprise, "Turn the other cheek," he
says, citing the wise.

But the reverend, with a harsh
tone, retorts, In Luke 22:36, a
verse he supports.
"He who has no sword, let him sell and buy one,"
To protect themselves, the congregation's champion.

A faint smile graces Captain
Effiong's face, Mocking the
reverend's misguided embrace.
"How much did your swords
cost?" he inquires, "Your hypocrisy
reeks," he subtly fires.

But he clarifies, not here to judge,
He seeks confession, not holding a
grudge. "Tell your men to drop
their weapons," he says, "We
come in peace, let peace guide our
ways."

But the reverend, standing

strong and bold, Refuses to
yield, his spirit untold.
"If you come in peace," he firmly demands,
"Put down your guns, leave my house, disbands."

Captain Effiong, still with a smile serene,
Questions the reverend's so-called
trained machine. "Are they truly
trained?" he calmly asks,
His doubt growing, behind a gentle mask.

The reverend, his tone
beginning to soften, Sees the
futility, aggression aloft in
coffin. "Captain," he starts, a
plea in his voice, "Drop your
weapons, let us make a
choice."

An insult, Captain Effiong
rightly sees, Guns
pointed at him, causing
unease.
"Tell your men to drop their weapons,"
he repeats, An olive branch extended,
peace it greets.

Fifteen

REVEREND'S STAND

The sentry officer, Captain
Effiong by name, Engages the
reverend in a dangerous game.
Pleading for security, his life to
be spared,
And the lives of his family, their souls ensnared.

"How can that be possible?" the captain asks,
Doubt and suspicion hidden behind his
masked tasks. But the reverend, restless
and unsure,
Whispers a secret plan, a desperate allure.

"I can pay you," the
reverend proposes, Hoping
to find a solution that
opposes. The sentry officer,
a giggle on his lips,
Wonders if this offer can reverse their eclipse.

But the captain ponders, pausing
to think, Deliberating the
reverend's offer, on the brink. He
agrees, but with due process in

play, Questions to be asked, the
price to pay.

The reverend requests the
questionnaire to see, To navigate
this dangerous decree.
"Do you accept Jesus Christ?" the
captain starts, A simple question,
but it tears their hearts.

"If you say 'Yes,' you die," the
captain reveals, But if you say
'No,' a chance for life appeals. The
reverend, torn between faith and
survival, Weighs his options, in a
treacherous arrival.

"Please, Captain, don't let me say
'No!'" he pleads, His voice trembling
with fear, his heart in need.
The captain urges him, "Then say
'Yes' instead, Embrace your faith,
let life be led."

But the reverend hesitates, unsure
and scared, Caught between the
choices, unprepared. "Why are
you doing this?" he cries in
despair, Putting him on the edge,
testing what's fair.

The captain insists, a simple

question to pose, "Yes" or "No,"
the answer life or death shows. The
reverend realizes the weight of his
decision, The gravity of the
moment, his soul's collision.

"I can't be in your shoes," the captain
remarks, For he's not the reverend,
caught in these sparks. The choice is
theirs, freedom to decide,
To stand with Christ or cast faith aside.

But the captain issues an order grim,
Those who stand with Christ will face
a dark hymn. He signals the soldiers,
their guns aimed high, Pointed at the
reverend, his fate drawing nigh.

Fear grips the reverend, his
voice trembling, A plea for
mercy, his soul resembling.
"Please, Captain, spare my life,"
he implores, But the captain's
resolve, his heart ignores.

"Are you for Jesus or against?"
he demands, In a voice that
echoes, his patience disbands.
Tears stream down the
reverend's face,
As he makes his choice, his faith's disgrace.

"I...choose to live," the
reverend admits, His voice
quaking, his heart torn to
bits. But the captain,
unsatisfied with his plea,
Denounces his answer, truth they must see.

Bursting into tears, the
reverend confesses, His heart
shattered, his faith in
distresses. "I am not for Jesus,"
he cries in despair,
"I want to live," his soul laid bare.

Sixteen

THE SHOCKING TRUTH

The room is filled with sorrow
and dread, The wife and
children, tears freely shed. Led
in by soldiers, frightened and
weak, Their hearts heavy,
voices unable to speak.

Soldier Four, forceful and rough,
Pushes them down, treating them tough.
Caught sneaking out, through the
back they tried, Their fate uncertain,
as fear fills each stride.

Reverend pleads, "Deal gently," he implores,
But the sentry officer corrects,
stating his scores. Addressed as
Captain Effiong, his title held high,
No room for error, no room for a lie.

Reverend interjects, answering
for his kin, "They are not dying,"
he claims, his voice thin. But the
sentry officer stands firm,
unbending, Each must answer,

their own faith defending.

Facing the reverend's wife with a
stern tone, The sentry officer lays
the truth, firm as stone. A
cleansing, he claims, wiping
Christians away, For their
fanaticism, they now must pay.

Rev. Mrs. stands strong, her voice
unwavering, Denying Christ earns
not life, she's savoring.
Quoting the Bible, she
counters their claim, Eternal
life, she proclaims, in Jesus'
name.

But the sentry officer reveals the truth,
Her husband made his choice,
denying the proof. Rev. Mrs. is
shocked, disbelief in her eyes,
Her heart shatters, her world filled with cries.

"No, it is impossible," she pleads in
despair, Praying her husband's
denial is just a nightmare. Eric
Godsman, she calls out to him,
Hoping it's all a joke, reality dim.

But Reverend stands silent,
unable to speak, His gaze fixed,
his spirit feeling weak.

Rev. Mrs. weeps, tears
streaming like rain, Her
husband's denial inflicting
deep pain.

In the room filled with anguish and despair,
Rev. Mrs. confronts her husband, her
 heart laid bare. "Eric, you betrayed Him,
 you nailed Him again,
For fear of death, you let your faith wane."

"You taught us the Bible, the
doctrines so true, You taught of
God, and His love that's imbued.
What happened to you? How did you
lose your way? Eric, tell me, please,
what led you astray?"

The sentry officer interrupts with a firm
tone, Confession time is near, their fate
to be known.
The teenage children, tears streaming
down their face, Stand by their mother,
embracing God's grace.

"As for me and my house, we
serve the Lord, In this generation,
we stand firm and restored. We
will not deny Him, we'll uphold His
name, Even in the face of death,
we won't be tame."

The sentry officer questions their
decision once more, To make them
reconsider, their faith to explore.
But Rev. Mrs. and her children,
resolute and strong, Stand together,
singing a courageous song.

Through tears and sorrow, their
voices rise, Recalling the martyrs
who met their demise. They
pledge allegiance to the Lamb,
their King, Unyielding in faith, His
praises they sing.

But the sentry officer, his
countenance changing, Turns his
back, his emotions rearranging.
A heaviness fills the room, silence
hangs in the air, As soldiers raise their
guns, a chilling glare.

Rev. Mrs. and her children kneel
down in prayer, Their hearts
steadfast, their souls aware.
The officers open fire, their shots
echoing loud, Their bodies fall, a
crimson shroud.

Reverend, in anguish, raises a sorrowful cry,
His heart shattered, tears streaming
from his eye. In that tragic moment,
lives given for their belief, Their

sacrifice, a testament to unwavering
grief.

The sentry officer blows his whistle, his
voice subdued, As Soldier 4 salutes, his
concern renewed.
"Sir, are you okay? You don't
seem fine, Please, talk to me,
share your troubled mind."

The sentry officer gazes into
the distance, A deep sigh
escaping, his inner resistance.
"I knew that woman once, in
days of old, But now, I must
obey, my duty unfolds."

Soldier 4 empathizes,
understanding the weight, A
problem shared, an alleviated state.
"Sir, have faith, you'll find
solace in time, You'll be
alright, your spirit will
climb."

As the people receive the CFI mark,
they're affirmed, The sentry officer
commands them, his voice firm.
"Embus," he declares, a directive clear,
Their paths diverge, each with their own fear.

Reverend, his tears flowing unabated,

Turns, unable to face the woman
he berated. "What have I done?
Denying the Lord's name, Fear of
death overshadowing my claim!"

His voice trembles as he utters a
desperate cry, "I am for Jesus
Christ! I'm willing to die!
He's my Savior, my guide, my eternal light,
I repent of my denial, my heart takes flight!"

But the guards have departed, leaving
him behind, Reverend's lament
echoes, his anguish combined. Yet,
from above, angels descend with
grace,
To escort Rev. Mrs, her children, and guards to a heavenly
place.

Seventeen

ELDER MACAULAY

In a spacious living room, so
finely furnished, An elderly man
sits calmly, undisturbed.
Late fifties, wise and dignified,
Facing the closed door, where troubles hide.

Beside him rests a Bible,
words divine, A glass of
water, tranquil and
benign. With crossed legs
and a peaceful gaze, He
sips his water, lost in
sacred ways.

But sirens wail, police cars approach,
Yet the old man's composure they fail
to encroach. He awaits the door's
opening with poise,
For he knows what awaits, the noise.

And with a resounding bang, the
door is shook, Soldiers enter, their
stance firm and hooked.
Major Collins steps forward, with purpose

in his stride, To cleanse the society of
religious pride.

"I am Major Collins," he declares
with pride, "Commissioned to rid
confusion far and wide. Pastor
Macaulay, it's your confession we
seek, To expose the truth, the
secrets you keep."

But Macaulay, unmoved,
simply smiles, Patiently
waiting, calmness for miles.
"For hours I've waited," he
calmly states,
While Collins and soldiers assume their postures,
straight.

"We've been to your church,"
Collins retorts, His voice laced
with an air of retorts.
But Macaulay interjects, his voice
cutting through, "My wife was shot,
by your hands, it's true."

"She made her choice," Collins retorts
with disdain, "We're sorry we couldn't
prevent her pain."
"She waits for me by the river,"
Macaulay shares, His faith
unwavering, casting aside all snares.

Mockingly, Collins adds
with a sneer, "In the
church, her blood did
smear, Not by the river,
as you believe,
Her final resting place, we did conceive."

Undeterred, Macaulay speaks
with grace, Unveiling truths
in the heavenly embrace. He
describes mansions, streets
of gold, The eternal glory, yet
untold.

"The Age of the Millennial, Christ's
divine reign, Believers united,
forever to sustain.
The New Earth and Heaven, void of
all woe, Where joy eternal, our
spirits shall bestow."

But Collins, in doubt,
questions the real, "Do
these places exist, or is it
zeal?" Macaulay, unfazed,
meets his gaze,
"And Officer Collins, are you real, always?"

Collins, taken aback, unsure what
to say, Knows his own existence
cannot be put at bay. And
Macaulay, seizing the moment,

proceeds, With a question that no
one heeds.

"What if this is my last
wish, my plea? Before you
pose your question to me,
Let me ask you, Officer
Collins, I insist,
Where shall you reside in your eternal twist?"

His words stir unrest,
unsettling their core, Soldiers
shift, a disquiet they can't
ignore. "Do these religious
tales hold your trust?"
Collins queries, doubting, his faith turns to dust.

"Is it Illogical," Macaulay imparts,
"That offenders face consequence for their
false starts? If criminals face justice in our
earthly domain,
Why disregard judgment in the spiritual plane?"

Collins, taken aback,
considers this view,
Analytical regulations,
familiar and true. Macaulay
continues, unveiling the
divine, Of sin and
redemption, a path so fine.

But Collins, uninterested, dismisses the

thought, Unyielding to the message that
Macaulay has brought. Until a sentry
officer, breaking the scene,
Interrupts, his voice firm and keen.

"I am interested in Jesus," he
declares, Startling the soldiers,
their surprise in the air. Collins,
furious, questions his sanity,
As the soldier unveils his own calamity.

"I ordered the killing," he confesses,
tears in his eyes, Of someone from his
past, a painful disguise.
Moved by the love he witnessed,
standing so tall, He wants to follow
Jesus, embrace His call.

Collins, in shock, his gun at the
ready, Demands clarification,
his voice steady.
And the soldier, trembling, utters
with might, "Jesus is my Lord,
my guiding light."

Collins, filled with rage, points the
gun so near, He demands the
soldier's faith to be made clear.
With a trembling voice, the soldier
finds his plea, "My Lord, my Savior,
Jesus, save me."

A gunshot echoes, the soldier falls,

The room consumed by
darkness, its walls. And
Collins, resolute, turns to
Macaulay, To take his
confession, no time for delay.

But Macaulay, undeterred,
begins to sing, A hymn of
hope, his heart taking wing.
"Gather at the river, beautiful
and divine, Where saints shall
meet, by God's design."

In his chair, he sinks, blood
staining his chest, A martyr's
end, he meets his final test.
Collins, victorious, his
mission complete, Yet in the
silence, a whisper of defeat.

Eighteen

THE BLOODED SANCTUARY

In a sanctuary filled with faithful
souls, Where prayers ascend
and devotion unfolds, A group
of believers fervently sing,
Their voices rising, their praises taking wing.

"We are soldiers, Soldiers of the Lord,
In the name of Jesus, we shall
conquer," they roar, Led by their 2IC, a
soldier so stern,
Marching through the crowd, military music's churn.

"Kill them, go kill them, go," they
chant with might, With unwavering
faith, they're ready to fight, "Only one
body," their voices resound,
Unified in purpose, their spirits tightly bound.

Surrounding the believers, the soldiers take
their stance, As they all hold on, in one
accord they advance,
Their mission clear, to cleanse the land,
Of fanatical religious groups, they take their stand.

2IC Collins, the voice of authority and
dread, Addresses the crowd, his words
piercing like a thread, "Ladies and
gentlemen, be aware of the law,
Cleansing this land, from beliefs we
abhor."

"Arise on your feet," he commands
with resolve, "To take your
confession, let the truth be solved,
Stand for Jesus, and you shall surely
die,
Deny Him, and you may live, no need to ask why."

As one, the believers rise, their
spirits unshaken, Their faith tested,
yet unbroken, unshaken,
2IC Collins, fighting his conscience within,
"I have killed tons of Christians today," his voice thin.

"This is the way I wanted to
be," he cries, His conflicted
soul tormented by lies,
But others join in, echoing the chant,
"I want to be a soldier," their voices enchant.

"Eeee, I want to be a soldier," they
sing with zeal, Their devotion
unyielding, a faith they reveal,
The leader steps forward, his
presence so grand, "This is the way I
wanted to be," he commands.

"To proclaim Jesus as Lord, as
King, as God, This is the path I
willingly trod,"
The crowd joins in, their voices
intertwined, "This is the way we
wanted to be," they find.

In the face of opposition,
they stand tall, Embracing
their faith, surrendering all,
But 2IC Collins, his anger
ablaze, Silences their song
with a furious gaze.

"Quiet!" he screams, his rage on display,
"Did I put the song in your mouth?" he
tries to sway, "You are playing with
fire," his voice resounds,
A warning to those who dare to astound.

And in the midst of the tension, a
question is posed, "Is there anyone
among you who wants to be closed, To
the idea of living?" Collins inquires,
A glimmer of hope, as silence transpires.

But the believers,
unwavering and strong,
Stand united, their conviction
prolongs,
For in their hearts, they've found

their true worth, To live for Jesus, the
King of all the Earth.

Their faith, unyielding, they
hold on tight, Ready to face
the darkness, ready to fight,
In unity, they remain,
steadfast and true,
For they know their purpose, their mission in view.

Nineteen
EMBRACING SALVATION

In a moment of rage, 2IC Collins fumes,
Grasping the leader, pinning him to the floor
with gloom, "How dare you interrupt me?"
he exclaims,
His anger consuming him, fueled by flames.

To his soldiers, he commands with urgency,
"Form a perimeter! Trigger on squad,
can't you see? Rain bullets on the
believers, standing there, Except the
leader, show him no mercy, be aware."

As the bullets rain down, merciless and grim,
Collins watches, weakened, as the
believers' lives dim, But the leader, in fear,
screams prayers to the sky, Seeking mercy
for his sins, tears flowing from his eyes.

"Lord Jesus, have mercy," he cries
out loud, Confessing his sins, his
hidden sins now unshroud, An
unrepentant sinner, masking his
shame, Praising on the surface, but
with a heart stained.

"What can wash away my sin?" he
begins to sing, Seeking redemption,
forgiveness it will bring, Nothing but
the blood of Jesus, he proclaims,
Yearning for the grace that only His
blood sustains.

Oh, precious is the flow that makes him
white as snow, No other fount he knows,
but Jesus, he does show, Amidst the
chaos, Collins signals his men to retreat,
Moved by the song, the scene now
bittersweet.

The leader, raising his head, watches
them depart, Confused, he calls out,
tugging at their heart,
"Officer, officer, where are you going? I'm
not yet slain," But Collins refuses, setting
him free from his pain.

A private officer, sensing the
rebellion's weight, Sends a signal,
a message of urgency and fate,
To reach the Area Commander, the
truth to unveil, A revolt in progress, a
truth they cannot fail.

Still on his knees, the leader pleads and implores,
To go home, to see his Lord, he longs for
those shores, The only place of safety, in

the presence of his God,
He begs the officer, commanding his men, a simple nod.

But Collins, breaking down, his voice
full of despair, Declares, "No, brother,
I can no longer bear,
To command the killing, to take more lives,
I'm tired, exhausted, the weight no one survives."

The leader, shocked by this
unexpected change, Asks, "Why?
Why now?" as emotions range,
Collins, sobbing, reveals his weary
soul,
"I've seen the difference, between dying for Him
and living for self, my role."

"I've witnessed people's smiles as they
meet their fate, Singing and dancing,
eager to reach heaven's gate, Only a few
foolish ones fear the loss of life,
While I, full of evil, sought power and strife."

Envy now seeping through, Collins
questions his worth, Can his wretched soul
find redemption, a new birth?
The leader, still on his knees,
imparts the truth, Of Jesus'
sacrifice, His love for all, resolute.

"He came to shed His blood, to
redeem us from sin, To save the world,

to let new life begin,
For God so loved the world, the
Scripture proclaims, Believe in Him,
eternal life it claims."

But Collins, burdened by his godless
acts and shame, Wonders if he's already
condemned, a life in vain, The leader
assures him of God's saving grace,
That through confession, forgiveness he'll embrace.

With Romans 10:8-11, the leader shares the key,
Confess with your mouth, believe in your heart,
you'll be free, For whoever believes will not be
put to shame,
Eternity's choice, heaven or hell, it will proclaim.

Collins, facing his comrades, asks if they
too are willing, To accept Jesus as their
Savior, their lives fulfilling,
Hesitant, two soldiers step forward, signifying
their choice, To embark on a new path, to let
their hearts rejoice.

The leader, filled with hope, kneels
before them all, Joined hands, a circle
formed, as they heed the call, Can you
say these prayers after me, he implores,
To accept Jesus, their Lord, their lives now restored.

In unison, they repeat the words with
conviction, Confessing their sins, seeking

eternal benediction,
As they invite Jesus into their hearts, a divine
connection, Their souls saved, bound
together in resurrection.

Twenty

VICTORY'S CHORUS

In a moment of stillness, a trumpet's
call resounds, The Area commander
enters, his presence astounds, Officers
who were kneeling spring up to their
feet,
But 2IC Collins, in shock, remains on his knees,
incomplete.

The commander questions, puzzled by the
sight, Where is his compliment? He seeks
answers with might, Stammering, Collins
rises, dons his cap, and salutes, Attempting
to regain composure, his actions acute.

The commander wonders, curious
about the scene, What had led his 2IC
to kneel, to intervene,
Collins stammers, explaining their
newfound faith, They had given their lives
to Jesus, a moment of grace.

The commander's voice booms,
shouting in disdain, Reminding Collins
of the rules, his words a strain,

Accepting Jesus means death, denying Him, a
chance to live, The commander demands
immediate confession, the truth to give.

Scared and trembling, Collins acknowledges
Jesus' name, While the leader interjects,
changing the aim,
He explains the contrary, the choice that
lies ahead, Accept Jesus, live forever; deny
Him, face eternal dread.

Quoting John 3:36, the leader presents the
truth, Believe in the Son, find everlasting
life, the eternal truth, But without belief,
the wrath of God remains,
A decision to be made, life or eternal fiery pains.

Enraged by the interruption, the
commander takes aim, Pulls out his pistol,
shooting the leader, a life he claims, Tears
flow from the soldiers, grieving their loss,
Collins falls to the ground, fearing the impending cross.

Amidst the fear and chaos, one soldier
softly sings, Of Jesus' love, the
assurance that it brings,
The melody carries, echoing
through the air, A reminder of
faith, a solace in despair.

On the ground, Collins prays, seeking
forgiveness, For his past, his

blasphemy, his soul's darkness,
He pleads with Jesus, his words filled
with remorse, Begging for mercy, a
chance to change his course.

The commander, disappointed, harbors anger
deep inside, He shoots Collins and the two
officers, their fate beside, Embus, he
commands, as he ends their lives,
Leaving behind a trail of sorrow, no chance to survive.

The brigadier band rises, playing a
solemn tune, Lifting the sleeping saints,
their spirits to commune, The music
weaves a sense of hope and solace,
As a banner emerges, bearing the words "Salvation is
for all" with grace.

In the midst of it all, the sentry officer stands,
Meeting Collins with a full complement and
loving hands, Bound together in faith, in the
face of adversity,
They find strength and unity, clinging to the melody.

The music persists, its message
strong and clear, "We shall
overcome," it sings, dispelling fear,
A chorus of voices rises, declaring
victory's call, Salvation is for all, a
truth that echoes for all.

End Note

In the darkest hour, when danger
draws near, A gun to your head,
filling hearts with fear.
Execution stakes, where life
hangs on thread, Soldiers of the
Anti-God, rifles widespread.

Children of the Kingdom, their
allegiance denied, In offices and
workplaces, where truth is defied.
Ashamed to bear the King's name, they
shrink away, Inferior, uncomfortable,
their faith held at bay.

Unwilling to raise the Flag of their
salvation high, They falter when
called upon, their loyalty awry.
Among the police force, betrayers
they dwell, Traitors to the Master,
their actions foretell.

In the civil service, rebels with a discontented
soul, Turning against the Kingdom, for a
morsel they enroll. Defectors and deserters,

embracing the wicked's stream, Abandoning
the Lord, in immorality they teem.

Planted by God across nations, His
children abound, To shine the light,
where darkness is found.
Provisions of light, abundant and bright,
Yet many lamps are hidden, devoid of their might.

When hands unite for evil, the Master
they betray, Deliberate sins, a path
they choose to stray.
Against the Kingdom's cause, rebels they
become, Abandoning their race, living by sinful
desires, numb.

Amidst the persecutions, some
believers stand tall, Dying for their
faith, never to let it fall.
Yet others compromise, without guns to
their name, Traitors, betrayals,
deserters, fueling the shame.

Standing down in the darkest
night's embrace, Their faith
dimmed, leaving no trace.
But hope remains for all to find their way,
To rekindle the light, for a new dawn's display.

From Darkness to Dawn

In the darkest of nights, a wailing
wind does blow, A trial unfolds, as
our hope takes flight, aglow.
When those deemed mighty start to
crumble and sway, The weaklings rise,
standing firm, come what may.

Amidst the chaos, a question arises,
cutting deep, Will you deny your faith,
or your conviction keep? In the face of
adversity, will you stand tall,
Or succumb to fear and watch your faith fall?

The night hangs heavy, casting shadows
far and wide, Whispering doubts creep
in, like a treacherous tide.
But in the hearts of the faithful, a fire burns bright,
A beacon of light that guides them through the night.

In the distance, the mighty stumble and
lose their way, Their thrones crumble,
their power begins to decay.
Yet, among the weaklings, a resilient
spirit ignites, They find solace in unity,

banding together in rights.

The choice is now yours, to
deny or to stand, To let faith
guide your steps, hand in hand.
For in the crucible of struggle,
character is revealed, And the truth of
your beliefs, boldly unsealed.

Will you falter, bowing down to fear's cruel sway,
Or rise above, embodying courage on this
fateful day? The strength of your
conviction shall be put to the test, In the
battle of faith, where hearts and souls
invest.

But fear not the darkness that
engulfs the night, For within you
lies a spark, a guiding light.
Let it blaze forth, illuminating your way,
As you navigate the trials, no matter what they weigh.

Stand firm, oh faithful soul, with
unwavering might, As doubts and
temptations try to dim your sight.
The darkest night shall pass, yielding to
dawn's embrace, And in the aftermath, your
faith shall find its place.

So, in this wailing night, hold onto hope's
fragile thread, With steadfast resolve, let
not your faith be misread.

For when the mighty fall and the weaklings
stand strong, You have the power to choose
where you belong.

www.ingramcontent.com/pod-product-compliance
Lightning Source LLC
Chambersburg PA
CBHW020537160726
47991CB00002B/471